BIRDIES & SAN DIEGO HEAT

A Roc Reese Mystery

OTHER BOOKS BY DUKE CHARLES

LUKE KASH WESTERN SERIES

People of the Horse
Spirit and the Blood
Blood and Thunder
Thunder Cloud and Spirit Walker

ROC REESE MYSTERY SERIES

Birdies and San Diego Heat
Birdies and Vegas Heat
Birdies and Texas Heat
Birdies and New Orleans Heat

Gideon, Bounty Hunter
Duke Charles' Shorts
Duke Charles' Shorts-Another Stinkin' Pair

When I Grow Up I Want To Be A Cowboy
Written with Brad Engel

BIRDIES & SAN DIEGO HEAT

A Roc Reese Mystery

DUKE CHARLES

Birdies & San Diego Heat

For information about this title or to order other books and/or electronic media, contact the publisher:

D C Engel

Twin Eagle Promotions

El Paso, TX 79912

www.DukeCharles.com

TwinEaglePromo@sbcglobal.net

ISBNs for Birdies and San Diego Heat

Softcover: 978-0-9969673-5-8

eBook: 978-0-9969673-6-5

Printed in the United States of America

Cover and Interior design: Bethel1808

Dedication

To my daughter, Lisa;
my son, Brett;
and my son, Brad;
to my grandson, Stewart, (U.S. Navy);
my grandson, Aksel;
and my granddaughter, Lauren;
and to my two great-grandchildren,
Eleazar Gideon and Jaea Elizabeth;

I love you all,
Greatdaddygrandpa Duke

Acknowledgements

Many thanks to my bride, Corrine, for putting up with my nonsense for the last 150 years, and making me the man I am today.

And a special thanks to my son and daughter-in-law, Brad and Laura, for taking the bull by the horns and making this whole project happen, from editing to printing. It has been so much fun working with you and I hope we can do it again...'cause I have so many more books that need to be published. Break's over, back to work.

Very truly,
Duke

Table of Contents

Foreword

I have exactly thirty-seven books on golf on my shelves. Some, like my wife, would say that's a lot; others, not even close. As I looked at each book remembering the teachings I gleaned, I realized that every single golf book I have eventually comes back to the mental game. Finally, I have come across one that doesn't.

I have known Duke Charles for forty-six years and have had the pleasure of being taught all about golf by him. I picked up my first golf club when I was eight years old and still remember those deep, thoughtful words he said to begin my lifelong instruction,

"Hey, put that down. That's not a toy."

Okay, maybe that's just how I remember it, but golf was always a serious topic in my family. The first time I pounded my putter in anger into the green on the fifth hole at Santa Teresa Golf Club just outside of El Paso, I was taught about respect for this great game.

I grew up loving golf and anything related to it. Going to my grandparents' house on Sunday and watching Arnie and Jack, Seve and Lee, and all my heroes come alive on the TV…there was nothing better. My son grew up loving the same game, and eventually had the honor of learning from Grandpa Duke the same lessons I had received years before; but somehow, he came home with a Scotty Cameron putter. Huh?

When I picked up Duke Charles' first book, *People of the Horse*, I was blown away. I immediately got the rough draft of the second book, *Spirit and the Blood* and could not put it down. Then I came across The Roc Reese Mystery Series. This may be the best golf book I have ever read. I know it's not a golf book in the normal sense of the word, but I identify with Roc. I understand the calling of the fairway and the therapy of the greens. I love reading about the action, the drama, the romance and especially the mystery that Duke has put together here.

Already a popular western writer, it shouldn't be a shock that Duke is able to put on paper such a great story that combines the most popular sport in the world with incredible action scenes, beautiful women and sunsets to die for.

Who says you can't have it all?

Brad Engel

Prologue

When I was 34 I birdied eight of the last nine holes for one of my biggest paydays. Not my biggest, but one of. Why didn't I play the tour? Well, I tried, but according to the powers that be, I wasn't the kind of person that would represent the PGA to the standard they set. They didn't say that exactly, but what else could it be. What? John Daly's alcohol and drugs and Boo Weekly's grasp of the English language; they at least tried to hide it and act the part. I don't. I live life by my rules and I'm actually okay with that.

My lust for the opposite sex and taste for distilled beverages was too legendary to hide from the public. And the fact that I have never been an early riser or very good at taking direction or following instructions, all collaborated against me and kept me from calling myself a professional golfer. Although, since I was a sophomore in high school back in 1970, I have never done anything for a living but play golf.

Hole 1
Reading the Greens

Tuesday morning, San Diego, Ca.

I was sitting on the small patio of my condo watching the surf as the rising sun was already reflecting off the water. With a cup of joe and a bowl of fresh fruit in front of me, I was trying to decide whether to take the kayak out or go for my half mile run, or maybe use the weight machines in the condo's exercise room. The phone rang. I looked at my watch, 7:47. The number on the caller ID was familiar but I couldn't put a face to it. The mind is starting to slip just a bit on occasion.

"This is Roc!"

A very familiar voice came on the line.

"Hey big guy, it's JJ. What's up?"

"Hey! My friend, just sitting here trying to decide what to do to get my heart beating."

"Well, how about some white ball for couple of k?"

"Anytime," I replied. "When and where?"

"One o'clock at the Pacific Coast Sporting Club. A couple of high rollers I played with in a tournament last weekend think they're unbeatable."

"Are they our age?"

"Yeah, they're 60-something, maybe late 50s."

"Can they play?" I asked; my curiosity aroused.

"Well, I guess they can't be beat at their club and that's got their heads all swelled up, but I wasn't impressed with their games; pretty vanilla. You know, plunk, plunk down the middle. But I doubt they've seen anything like you up close and personal."

"I'll meet you at the diner in Encinitas at 11:30," I said and headed for the shower.

I pulled my 2008 Lexus LS460 onto the 5 and headed north. I had just retrieved it from the neighborhood paint shop a couple of days earlier and it looked like a brand spanking new car. What we called Candy Apple Red when I was a kid in high school. The 90,000 miles on the odometer didn't bother me. These cars run forever and this one looked perfect, inside and out.

Forty two miles from my condo to Candy's diner in the seaside town. I parked beside JJ's two year old Jaguar convertible coupe; white, with black leather interior.

I walked inside just as my cell phone vibrated; it was JJ telling me he was here. I sat down in the booth while he was waiting for me to answer.

“How do you do that? You're always sneaking up on me.”

“Mr. Reese, so good to see you again,” the waiter said. “Your usual?”

“Yeah, Billy...that’ll work and water with lime.” Billy left to place my order.

My usual was a BLT and a small bowl of Clam Chowder.

JJ and I made small talk for a few minutes.

“So what’s the deal, Kiddo?” I asked.

JJ was 2 or 3 years younger than me. He had silver hair and always dressed to the nine’s, looked like he stepped out of a men’s fashion magazine, even after spending all day on the course. I always thought I looked pretty good till I met up with him. Compared to JJ, I looked like a homeless guy. He’s got a 32 inch waist; I have a 34, with just a little gut. His hair never seems to move; my thinning hair always looks like I have a hair dryer permanently attached to my shoulder. And I couldn’t have got the crease in my pants that sharp or my shoes to shine like that if I had stayed up all night and worked on them, which of course, I wouldn’t.

“$500/Press when you’re pissed!” JJ said.

“Any strokes?”

“Nah! They don’t think they need any and I sure didn't offer. You remember the course?”

“Yeah, wide fairways, good greens, lots of water and not very long. I haven’t played it in a year or so, but it shouldn’t be a problem.”

I told JJ to handle the bets.

“Whatever blows your dress up is fine with me.”

JJ and I go way back. Been so long now, I'm not exactly sure how we met. He knows me and puts up with my crap. He's always had my back and I know I don't have to worry about money with him. Not sure he would take a bullet for me. He's just not that guy. But I can trust him. There's a huge value in knowing who you can trust.

I followed JJ down the hill to the parking lot of the Pacific Coast Sporting Club; a very exclusive golf course reserved for gentlemen only, or at the very least, grown men with some bucks.

I gave the kid that loaded our clubs a twenty and he started cleaning them. We hadn't hit a shot yet. I had to tell him to stop so we could drive off.

"You want to hit some balls?" JJ asked.

"Just a few, I only have so many swings before the back gives out."

JJ went into the pro shop and checked us in. There was no charge. We were the guests of Mr. Carlson.

I rolled half a dozen putts to get the speed of the greens and then we rode out to the driving range. Unlimited, almost new Titleist balls on the range.

"Lord, I love the rich."

I would have put some in my bag but my compartment was full. I had just bought a couple of dozen pre owned balls at the shop at my condo's pitch and putt course. Pity! Maybe on the way out.

Bob Carlson and Ray Benson were standing on the first tee acting perturbed for having to wait.

I looked at my watch. It was 12:50 and I thought, here we go!

"So where'd you go? Keep it in play?"

They just looked at each other.

"Uh, we haven't hit yet."

"Well, go ahead, you won the toss," I said with a smirk. Already in their heads. This may be easier than I thought.

Rey teed it up and pulled it into the left rough.

"I'm gonna hit a mulligan," and he took another ball from his pocket.

"Hey! I thought we were playing golf," JJ spoke up.

"Hit it, go find it and hit it again till it goes in the hole," he said.

Ray turned a little red, trying not to show his anger. Then Bob teed it up and hit driver down the fairway about 210. He was obviously the A player on the team.

JJ hit 3 wood about 195 with a little fade and it rolled into the first cut about 2 feet off the fairway. I hit a 3/4 driver that went up the middle. 230 with a slight draw but it stayed in the short grass, and we werc off.

They were up ahead of us and I kept seeing Ray turning and looking back. Then he would say something to Bob and then look back again.

I was singing a little Turtles ditty 'I'm a believer' and I think that bothered Ray even more. This was hard work for him. Just another day in Paradise for me and JJ, his eyes straight ahead as usual.

Ray rolled his second shot about 80 yards up the fairway and JJ hit a five iron that stopped just short of the green about 30 feet from the pin. Ray hit his 3rd, a decent shot that made the right side of the green about 20 feet away.

Bob took a couple of practice swings and then hit a five iron that skidded and rolled past the flag about 25 feet. I had 133 to the flag and I pulled a nine from my bag. From watching Bob's shot I could see the green was a little firm, so I choked down about an inch, opened the face a little and hit down on the ball. I swung a little harder than I like to. It went high and landed soft about fifteen feet short and rolled to within eight feet of the flag.

JJ looked at me and smiled. I missed my birdie, kind of on purpose.

Bob lagged up close and we gave him his par while Ray picked up after 5 and put it in his pocket. All square.

I asked JJ on the way to the second tee, "Is that as good as they get?"

"That's about it for Ray. Bob can be a little stronger but he won't be under par when it's over."

"Who will?" I asked.

"Yeah, Yeah! You can be if you need to be.

"Well, I hope I don't need to, so maybe these guys will want a rematch."

I missed the green on two, but JJ made a twenty foot snake for a half. The third was a par three over the water. JJ gave me a wink so I hit a nine iron 134 yards about five feet from the hole and made the birdie for a one up lead.

On eight they pressed. I guess they thought they had us figured out.

JJ rolled one off the tee and every one laughed, until I drilled one 250 in the heart of the fairway. Bob hit his best shot. Came out of his shoes and he was twenty five yards behind me. I knew it was over.

They pressed again on nine and they lost that hole as well. We were up $1500 and Bob and Ray were pissed.

"Hey Reese! What's your handicap anyway?" said Ray.

"I thought we were playing straight up?" I replied. "My card says 4."

Ray got a little uppity, "Your one under on the front."

"Is that right? I wasn't counting," I said with a grin. "It's bound to fade, it always does."

"That's a bunch of bull!"

His partner tried to calm him down but Ray was starting to feel the heat.

Bob said, "Will you boys accept a press?"

"Sure. Play the back for a grand?"

"And make the presses a grand too!" Ray said. Then he looked me in the eye.

"Don't I know you?"

"Maybe, I've been living on the coast since I got out of the service in '77," I replied.

"What do you do?" Ray asked.

"About what?" I said with a smirk.

"What do you do for a living?"

"My wife left me pretty well off."

"From what?" he asked.

"She was a real expensive hooker in Hollywood and she saved her money."

JJ looked at me and shook his head.

"You my friend are a real asshole. Jeanie would not have thought that was funny," he half-whispered.

"Well, she's not here anymore, and please don't tell her if you see her soon."

Jeanie was the only woman I had ever loved. Not made love to, but truly loved. She died of cancer two years earlier. It was hard to tell exactly what kind because she was eaten up by it. She was only sick for about 6 months. She went really fast...too fast.

I stunk up the first three holes on the back and acted like I was really pissed. JJ won the first two and lost the third. We were one up. Bob and Ray had kind of forgotten about me and were trying to gang up on JJ; dropping clubs in the middle of his swing, coughing, farting and just about every juvenile thing they could come up with. It was just too obvious. I parred the thirteenth and halved it with Bob. They felt pretty sure they had us on the ropes.

"What do ya think, Bubba?" I asked JJ. "You ready to get this thing over with? I'm ready for a little more than Gatorade. My flask is dry and these guys are starting to get on my nerves."

"Okay. But try not to make it look to obvious, will ya?"

I birdied fourteen and chipped one in from the fringe on fifteen for par and halved the hole, we were two up with three to go.

"Press, Damn it! Press!" Ray was turning red.

Bob was being cool, but trying to figure out how they got in this position. It didn't look like either JJ or I was playing all that great, but here they were; two down and pressing and his partner was losing it.

On 15 JJ hit a decent shot about 220 in the right side of the fairway and I backed off and hit a 3/4 driver about 235 in play.

Ray swung so hard he almost whiffed the ball. He hit one of the biggest slice's I've seen in my 60 years. His ball crossed the 17th fairway and bounced on the cart path, over the fence and rattled around the front porch of a very nice, what I considered to be a mansion. Ten seconds later, an old man came out in his underwear, looked around, picked up Ray's golf ball, examined it and took it back into the house.

Ray was fuming. He swung his driver with all his might and misjudged the distance between him and his cart. He hit the aluminum bar that held the windshield in place and his club head snapped, sailing by Bob's head just as he was swinging. Bob topped the ball and it rolled about 75 yards. Ray's club head landed about 30 yard ahead of the tee box and Bob said with a straight face,

"That's the first time you've been in the fairway on the back side."

Ray looked like he was going to cry. He tried to break the headless driver shaft over his knee but he wasn't strong enough and it slipped out of his hand and hit him hard across the left side of his face. He sat down in the cart and tears were streaming down his face along with a long red welt that was rising rapidly. Was it the pain from the shaft, the embarrassment from the tee shot or breaking his club? Who knows, and really, who cares.

JJ won 16 with a par. Three and two, and they quit on the 17 tee box. They both dug in their bags and each counted out $3,500.

I told JJ to let me get mine from Ray, just to put the needle in a little deeper. I took the money with my left hand and shook Ray's hand a little harder than necessary and said, “Hey buddy, don’t let it get ya down, we've all been there!”

That just about pushed Ray over the edge. He walked away and tried to kick the cart as he went by, but hit the rear bumper with his ankle and I swear I heard it snap.

“Oh well! I guess you're out for tomorrow? Huh Ray!”I said as he limped off.

Bob was talking with JJ and as it turned out, he was in for tomorrow. He had made a call and got another one of his buddies to join him in the morning. He was convinced that he could have beat us if he only had a decent partner.

We were sitting at the bar of one of my favorite restaurants in Encinitas, looking out at the ocean, slurping on Crown Royal on ice and waiting for our Filet and Lobster platters to come out, when this 30-something, weight lifter, MMA star, prize fighter, etc. looking guy walked in. He took a bar stool one down from me and ordered a beer and a shot. He threw the shot down and chased it with a swallow of beer, then turned to me.

“Mr. Reese?”

I turned and said, “Yeah!”

“I’m Neil Benson.”

“That’s good. How you doin’, Neil?”

“Not so good,” he said.

“Sorry to hear that, Neil.”

People hate it when you over-use their name. I knew it. And this guy hadn’t done anything wrong yet, but I couldn’t help myself.

I continued, “My buddy and I are about to have a good meal. If you can change your mood, you’re welcome to join us.”

“Well, no sir. You see, my dad said you robbed him today.”

“Who did you say you are?”

“I’m Ray Benson’s son.”

I looked at JJ and asked, “Who the hell is Ray Benson?”

I knew who he was, but I wasn’t going to quit now.

“The guy we played today.” JJ said laughing under his breath.

“Oh! That Ray Benson. And what exactly is it you want me to do for you, Neil?”

“I want you to give my dad’s money back.”

“Your dad’s money?” I looked him in the eye for a couple of seconds. Then I asked, “Do you gamble Neil?”

“A little, in Vegas from time to time.”

“And when you lose, Neil, do they give you your money back?” I asked

“No sir!”

“No Neil, they don’t. In fact, if you lose enough, they give you a room and a meal to make you feel good, so you’ll lose some more. Right, Neil?”

“Yes sir.”

“Neil, would you like me to rent your dad a room and buy him a couple of McDonald's burgers?”

He stared at me, not sure if I was serious or not.

“I’m gonna have to ask you to give me the money, Mr. Reese.”

“Well, Neil, I’m going to sit here and eat my dinner and if you're still here when I’m through we can go outside and settle this like gentlemen. You hit me, I shoot you.”

Neil looked at me, not quite sure what to think. I picked up my drink with my left hand and raised the shirt tail of my Tommy Bahama camp shirt with my right exposing just enough of my Glock 26, 9mm to make sure ol’ Neil got a good look.

“You see Neil, I’m too old to fight, and too tired to run. So, if you persist in doing this stupid dance, I’ll be your partner but we won’t be going home together. Do you understand?”

“Yes sir, I do.”

“So Neil, what are you going to tell your Pop?” I asked.

“I gonna tell him, I asked, and you said no.” And he walked out the door leaving most of a full beer.

JJ had been looking at Charlie, the bartender, rolling his eyes and sipping his Crown during the whole thing. He turned to me and asked, “Are you still carrying that old shooter?”

“Actually, I’ve upgraded to a smaller version, a Glock 26. Only holds 10 rounds, but if I can’t get the job done with 9, I’ll put the 10th in my ear.”

JJ laughed, “Some things never change!”

I grew up around firearms. My dad, a Los Angeles policeman, taught me about all kinds of guns. We hunted and fished and we even tried to play some golf together when I started, but he just didn’t have the skills. He wasn’t bad, he just didn’t want to hold me back and when he saw my ability, he got me some professional instruction. An expense that I later realized he couldn't afford, mainly because of his addiction and affection for Irish whisky. I found out later that he drank on the job and usually went through a fifth or more a day, but I never saw him drunk. I guess maybe I never saw him sober, and apparently he never got caught. That may be where I got my taste for the drink.

"I'll meet you for lunch at Candy's tomorrow," I told JJ and then I headed down the coast. The sun was just setting and the colors were spectacular.

Hole 2
Let the Big Dog Eat

I walked through the club house heading for my condo and noticed Lisa May, part time girl friend, part time lover, part time pain in my ass. At sixty I just didn't require the companionship or the hassle of a full time relationship any longer.

"Hey, you want a drink?" she said.

I did, but alone on my patio.

"Uh... Sure. You want to come over? I need a shower. I'll leave the door unlocked."

We sat on my patio as the moon came up, and had too many Crowns. Or maybe it was the ice. Who knows, 'cause I don't remember going to bed or Lisa leaving.

She was sitting in the Rec Room drinking coffee with a couple of the other widows from the complex when I walked by.

"Good morning Ladies, beautiful day isn't it?" I said with my best hangover smile. Two of the ladies melted and said "Good morning Roc" with their biggest smiles, but Lisa just ignored me and I walked on by,

Well, at least I won't have to worry about entertaining her tonight. And I hit the road for Encinitas.

"Your usual, Roc?"

"Nah. I need four poached eggs on a couple of English muffins with some green chili and cheese on them, some hash browns and lots of coffee."

"You got it!"

JJ came in as I was about half way through my meal.

"Uh Oh! Long night?" he asked.

"No. Actually, a pretty short one. I don't remember much after nine o'clock."

"Aren't you getting a little old to hit it that hard?"

"You would think so. But it may be too late to stop now, besides, I don't remember starting."

I dumped all the balls from my bag into my trunk and reloaded at the driving range. Just something about paying $50 for a dozen golf balls that pisses me off, so I go for the pre-owned for $19 and these are even better, Free! Kind of silly when I'm playing for a $1000 five ways? Front, back and total and an auto press on each side.

"Okay," I said. "Let's dance."

Without boring you with too many details, the day went pretty much like the day before. We closed them out on 17 and drove to the clubhouse where they paid us at the bar. Bob and his new partner were a lot more amiable than ol' Ray the day before. They convinced each other that with just a little luck and one or two more good shots, they could of had us.

Not!

I put my bag full of almost new Titleist balls in my trunk and saw Neil walking my way. I unzipped the pocket where I kept my wallet, watch, car keys and Glock and laid my pistol beside my bag as I put my stuff in my pockets. Just in case.

I heard Neil say. "Mr. Reese! Can I have a minute of your time?"

I turned to face him, "Sure. What's on your mind, Mr. Benson?"

"I wanted to apologize for yesterday. I completely overreacted. I'm a little over protective of my pop, knowing full well that 99% of the time his problems are self inflicted."

"You're a good son, and I'm glad we didn't have to get serious about this."

"Well, I try, but he's a handful as you can tell."

"How's his ankle?" I asked.

"Broken!"

And we both had to laugh a little. We shook hands and Neil returned to caring for good ol' Ray.

JJ walked up and asked, "What was that all about?"

"Just Neil, giving me an update on his dad's medical condition. He won't be teeing it up for about six weeks."

"That's going to be funny for a long time."

"Sure is. Hey Pard, I'll talk to you soon," and I headed south towards home.

I got back into San Diego and decided I'd like some fried shrimp and a cold beer, so I turned right instead of into the parking lot of my complex.

My favorite restaurant is Jaxon's. A great view of the ocean, great seafood and ice cold beer and they were famous for their hot waitresses. Several of them had made it to Hollywood, and that made Mr. Jaxon kind of a celebrity in his own right. So he had the pick of the crop in San Diego for wait staff and believe me there was a great crop to pick from.

"Hey, Roc! What's up?"

"Hey, Lucy. Just another day in paradise."

"Coors light?" she said.

"Yeah, Why not? And a shot. Gotta start somewhere." I sat up at the bar 'cause it had a great view of the water and Lucy, without having to deal with the cooling breeze that came off the ocean this time of year on the outdoor patio.

I did the shooter and took a swallow of beer and said, "I'll have the shrimp with fries and a small salad with Roquefort."

"You taking me home tonight?" Lucy asked.

"Of course, but I probably better eat first." I said.

"You got it, Hun!" Lucy disappeared to the kitchen to place my order.

If only I could get so lucky. I'm not stupid; I know she is just flirting for a bigger tip, and yeah, she's gonna get a bigger tip.

I took a long swig of beer and tried to enjoy the sunset, but was interrupted when I felt a hand on my shoulder of a very pretty lady, maybe 40, maybe less.

"Are you Rocland Reese?"

"Uh, Yes, ma'am, I am. How can I service you? I mean, be of service."

"I'm Pat, Lisa's daughter."

"Nice to meet you, Pat. What's on your mind?"

"Have you seen my mom today?"

"Yeah. I saw her when I left this morning. She was in the club house having coffee with a couple of other gal's, why? What's up?"

"I have been trying to reach her since about 10:30 this morning and nothing. She never goes anywhere without her phone."

"Did you go by her house?" I asked.

"Yeah, I did. Her phone was there. Her purse and her car keys too."

"Lucy brought my meal, "Have you eaten today?"

"No. I haven't," she replied.

I had Pat help me eat my shrimp and spuds so we could start the search for her mom.

I ate the small salad with Roquefort myself, 'cause I wanted to.

We went back to the complex and talked to the two gals she was doing coffee with this morning. They both said she was going to do some shopping.

It was just a short walk from my complex to a strip center that had a grocery and other services; liquor, a couple of restaurants, beach wear for seniors, etc.

The food store and liquor store both said they knew who she was, but hadn't seen her today. The clothing store was closed and the restaurants had the evening shift working, so no help there.

We went back to the complex and got my car and drove south, down the coast highway. I tried to remember what she was wearing when I saw her that morning. Blue blouse? No...orange. And white slacks with orange sneakers, and her blond hair was up in a pony tail. I told Pat what to look for.

I called my drinking buddy at the SDPD.

"This is Chief Brown. How can I help you?"

"Dan, Roc here. I have a missing person. I know it's too soon to report, but if you could put an unofficial APB out I would truly appreciate it. Her name is Lisa May and she was wearing an orange blouse, white slacks and orange sneakers. And blond hair in a ponytail."

I asked Pat if she had a picture on her phone and she did.

"I'll send a picture to your phone. She was last seen about 10:30 this morning at my complex. Her phone, car keys and purse are in her condo."

"Okay, Roc, I'll look into it. I'll be in touch. You take care."

I told Pat that we might as well call it a night, if she calls we need to be by her phone. What I really meant was, if the kidnappers call we should be by a phone.

"Would you like a drink?" I asked.

"Oh Lord, I'd really love one," she said.

"Grab your mom's phone and come on over, I'll fix us a cocktail. What's your pleasure?"

"Whisky, on ice, if you have it."

"I have both, I think. Crown Okay?"

“Perfect, that’s my first choice,” she said.

My kind of gal, or girl, or do I have grandkids her age? Pretty close I would imagine.

We had a couple of drinks on my patio and made small talk. Then my cell phone rang.

“Hello. This is Roc.”

“Roc. It’s Dan.”

“Yeah, Dan. What’s up?”

“Got some bad news. The beach patrol just found a floater under the pier. No ID, but based on your description and her clothes, I'd say it’s her.”

“Wow! Okay. We’ll head for the precinct. See you in a few.”

I said to Pat, “I have some bad news for you.”

“What is it?”

“They found a body under the pier. 95 % certain it's your mom. I’ll drive you to the station.”

I really hate it when women cry, and I hate it even worse when I did nothing to cause the tears. It makes me feel really helpless.

I got Pat calmed, as much as possible, and we drove to the station just as the morgue van pulled up. I walked her inside and checked in at the desk, then walked back and sat down by Pat.

“They’ll call us when we can go in.”

She nodded.

Lisa was pretty torn up from the razor clams and mussels that grew on the columns under the pier, but it definitely was Lisa. I’m not sure that Pat had ever seen a dead person up close before. I had my arms around her and I felt her knees begin to give. I backed her up to a chair and helped her sit.

I asked the attendant if they had any idea of COD, and he said it looked like blunt force trauma to the right side of the head, but they'd know more after the autopsy, probably day after tomorrow. I thanked him and sat down beside Pat.

We got back to the complex and I asked if I could do anything. She said no, but that she was going to stay at her mom's condo for a few days and she would see me tomorrow.

I opened a beer and took a shower then put on some shorts and a comfy old sweatshirt and sat on the patio. I was there for about half a beer when the doorbell rang.

"Patricia? My dear, what is it?

"I could use a drink and a shoulder," she said.

She was wearing a terry cloth beach robe that stopped about mid thigh. I had seen it on her mom from time to time but believe me it looked much better on Pat. She had on heels, but as close as I could tell, that was all. Maybe she was so distraught she didn't realize what she was doing. Nah!

I poured her a very stiff Crown and a shot for myself to go with my beer. I handed her the drink and by the time I sat down and looked her way her glass was empty.

"Mind if I have another?"

She was already up and on her way to the bar.

"Uh, no...why don't you just bring the bottle back?"

She came back, sat and crossed her legs and one side of her robe fell away.

Crap! I did my best not to stare, but damn! Maybe she thought I was too old to be affected or notice. Wrong!

Pat brushed her long blond hair back from the side of her face with her left hand and raised her glass with her right and took a long pull.

"What do we do now?"

"We...uh, well, it's a murder case and it's in the hands of the police now."

"Did you know my mother was a very wealthy woman? And so am I."

"I wasn't sure, but from the way she dressed and lived I would guess she had money. But we never discussed it."

"Roc, I know you're probably busy, but I would feel much better if someone I knew was handling it. Is there any way you could look into this. Money's no object."

I had over $9,000 in cash in my golf bag and a pretty good chunk in the bank. I really didn't need any money at the moment.

"Pat, I think you have the wrong idea. I'm a golfer, not a cop or a private investigator."

"Please Roc. You knew her. The cops didn't. Besides, she really liked you. She talked about you all the time."

I'm not sure if it was the drink, the way she looked in that robe that was falling off or if she was actually that convincing, but something in me said of course I will."

"Let me make a couple of calls in the morning and see what I can find out," I said.

"Thank you, Roc. If it's okay, I'm just going to stay here. I don't want to be alone tonight."

Ah, Crap! But of course, she wasn't.

I'm not sure how old she was, but young enough to still look good in the morning. I felt like a 60 year old that needed a shave, a shower, a cup a Joe and some Tylenol Plus.

I talked to my friend, Chief Dan about 10 AM and he told me that someone saw her and a tall, young blond surfer type walking on the pier yesterday morning around eleven. He said it looked like the murder weapon was a 1 inch pipe.

I told Pat what I had found out and asked her what she wanted me to do?

"Just stay on top of things, will you? I don't want this to be swept under the rug."

"It won't be. This is a murder case and we don't have that much crime in the senior community. They should have the information on the news this morning."

I turned on a local channel. I wasn't sure if the 65 inch flat screen would even work. I couldn't remember the last time I had it on. Fortunately, it fired right up, I was almost surprised.

My icebox had beer, three slices of Godfather's pizza that was green beyond recognition, a bag of Cowboy coffee from Sam's and a container of pink grapefruit in light syrup. Pat took one look and decided we should go to the Rec room for breakfast. I concurred.

One of my golf buddies called as we were on our 3rd cup of coffee to see if I was going to make our regular Friday morning tee time. I had completely forgotten.

"I'm sorry, Pard. Something's come up. I have a friend that needs some help and I can't walk away."

"Good for you," my friend replied. "Let us know when you get free."

"Thanks, I will. Talk to you soon.

"Where do we go from here?" Pat asked.

"I think we should go for a walk on the pier and show her picture around to see if anyone remembers seeing her yesterday."

Pat looked amazing. A gray knit short sleeve sweater that looked like it had been spray painted on, navy blue slacks that had the crease professionally sewed in and navy blue sandals with just enough heel to give her that sexy walk.

We walked the pier and the regular fishermen were in their usual spots with their Yeti thermoses, Styrofoam cups, quarts of beer and paper sacks with God only knows what in them. I showed them a recent picture of Lisa that Pat had sent to my phone. Several folks remembered her but since she was a regular on the pier, they weren't sure if it was yesterday or the day before. A couple of people shared some vague information about a thirty-something surfer type that they thought might have been with her. Tall, long blond hair, tan, denim cut-offs, tank top with muscles and flip flops. A million five hundred thousand look-a-likes in San Diego, but not so much in our little corner of the world; Paradise, senior style.

We ordered a cup of coffee at the Plunge Inn; a fast food joint at the end of the pier. Place's like these used to be so exciting to me when I was a kid. Corn dogs, Burgers and fries and the salt air. But now it was just a dirty dive with Seagull crap on the cement tables and benches and the smell of burnt grease from the deep fryer.

The heavily tattooed guy behind the window with long stringy hair, a grungy apron and semi white tee shirt spoke first.

"What kind of coffee you want?"

"Preferably hot, if we have a choice," I replied and got one of those twenty-something looks like, hey man! What's your problem?

"What can I get your granddaughter?" he asked.

You smart ass little prick! I though it, but over the years I have found that it is best to hold my tongue in certain situations. Food prep tops my list. Besides, that is exactly what I would have said at his age. Hell, that's exactly what I would say now.

We got our coffees and then found a place at the rail to the side of the food shack that was the least visible from the window and that had a minimal amount of seagull crap. We found ourselves looking down at the rolling waves.

"This is probably where she went into the water," I told Pat.

The only time I spend on the pier is late at night when the weather is inclement. I love the ocean at its roughest. I truly enjoyed the nights at sea when I was a young Coasty sitting on deck and riding out a hurricane.

I started to put together a picture in my mind of what the killer might look like and what his motives might be. Lisa didn't have any money with her; nothing of value. It was all still in her condo. She owned a new 700 series BMW, and she probably had a ton of cash and jewelry around her house, so it wasn't a robbery. Was it anger or maybe just a random kill? Very strange! Why wouldn't the killer do someone more his own age, and in downtown San Diego where he could just disappear into the crowd? Something drew him to the senior community. Maybe the fact that we all had very short memories, and he could walk about without being noticed or at the very least, remembered.

I called Chief Dan and asked him if he had any more information he could share with me. I told him what we had found out. Pretty much the same as his guys.

Hole 3
In the Rough

By 1pm we had walked back to the condo and picked up Pat's car, she wanted to fill it up with gas and have it washed, I hadn't noticed it in the parking lot but it was a big, new Mercedes, I mean big, I guess I had never been inside or noticed how big the S550 sedan was, and extra Black. She wanted me to drive, wow! I thought my Lexus had whistles and bells but this thing was crazy, I'm guessing well over a 100 grand.

"Where's the espresso machine?" I asked.

"You'll need to pull over."

I started to, then asked, "Why?"

"Because it's in the trunk!"

We both smiled.

I was feeling like a 17 year old kid trying to get into the pants of the cutest cheerleader in high school.

"What's your plan?" she asked.

“Well, the cops have a lot more resources than we do, so I guess we’ll just do some cruising and see what we can see.”

Without much success I might add.

We had a few Crowns and water and an early dinner at Jaxon’s; Crab Cakes with a Caesar salad and Oysters Rockefeller and a couple of white wines. Just enough to get me feeling forty again.

We went back to the complex and Pat followed me into my place. It was beginning to look like I had a new room mate.

What did I do to deserve this; good or bad? I guess we’ll find out.

About 6:30 my cell phone rang.

“Hey Roc! It’s Dan.”

“Yeah Dan, What’s up?” I asked.

“They found another floater this afternoon, downtown. Same M-O, pipe mark and all.”

“Sounds like we might have a serial killer,” I said.

“Wait a second. It’s a big jump from same M-O to serial killer, and we don’t need any talk like that till we know for sure.”

“Okay, okay, where’s the body?”

“It’ll be at the morgue in about an hour.”

“Thanks Chief, I appreciate you keeping me in the loop. I’ll talk to you soon.”

I told Pat about the new murder and the resemblance in the two.

“Do you want to go with me to the morgue?” I asked.

“No. I’m wiped out. I’m going to stay here and take a hot bath.”

By here, did she mean here here or next door here? It should be interesting.

"Okay, I'll see you later," I said as I headed for my car, wondering if she would be here or at her mom's when I got back? I truly didn't mean to create this monster. As monsters go, this one really ain't all that bad, but if I told any of my golf buddies about her they wouldn't believe me. Oh well, guess I'll just play it where it lies and see what happens.

Chief Dan was still at the Station when I arrived and he greeted me with a handshake.

"I'm not sure if this will help, but this gal had a piece of cotton cloth in her hand; part of a tee shirt would be my guess. The lab's working on it now. This could be a break but it's a long shot that we'll find any DNA. We'll see."

We walked down the hall to the ME's office and then into the morgue. There she was lying on the stainless steel table. I was amazed at how much she resembled Lisa. Something is wrong here.

"Dan, did you take a look at Pat's mom when they brought her in?"

"No. Why?"

"Because this one could be her twin sister. What if these two weren't his first victims? What if he just changed his location 'cause things were getting a little warm somewhere else?"

"The serial killer theory again...okay, fine. Let me get some feelers out. I'll get back to you as soon as I hear something."

By the time I got back home it was 8:00. I had pretty much forgotten about Pat, when I walked into my condo and...I could smell scented candles and hear soft music playing. There she was in my Jacuzzi tub; bubble bath almost overflowing with nothing on but a big smile. Okay, I may be just a touch old for this. It's starting to be not as exciting as it was two days ago. My 'want to' was still hanging around but my 'can't' had pretty much taken over".

"Hey Rockland, would you bring the wine?"

"I'm having trouble just walking," I said to no one particular.

I grabbed the mostly empty white wine bottle from the cooler on the bar and poured the rest into her giant wine glass on the edge of my tub.

"You better open another one before you get in. I put a couple in the fridge to cool."

"Yes, Dear," I mumbled softly.

Here we go again. No matter how hot she is or how sweet she seems, some other guy has already had enough of her bull.

I pulled the cork and grabbed a very large glass of my own and headed for the bubbles. Being with her really wasn't that bad. Just kind of like a bath; not so hot once you've been in it for a while.

The next morning I felt like a piece of pasta; Al Dente. I made it from the bed, two steps to a chair and took a break. I wonder when she's going home. Not her mom's place but all the way home. I don't guess I ever asked or maybe I forgot where she really lives.

Pat was in my kitchen. She had poached eggs, ham buttered toast, cranberry juice and coffee.

"Where'd all this food come from?" I asked. I knew it wasn't from my ice box.

"I found it at mom's place. She's got a freezer full of filets and lobster and all kinds of stuff in her garage; enough to last a family of 10 a year or so."

"Uh, I don't usually eat breakfast unless I got bombed the night before."

"Yes, and...?" she said.

"Oh yeah. I see what you mean. It does smell pretty good."

It was good too. Where is she going with this? She can't just be being friendly. It ain't in their nature. Devious, cunning, sneaky, what else...? That's all I can think of at the moment with this headache. But you know what I mean.

"Where do you live? Did you ever tell me or have I just forgotten?"

"I don't think it ever came up. I have a condo up the road about 40 minutes in Capistrano."

"Any pets or boy friends?" I asked.

"No. Just you." she said.

Crap! I really don't want to be in this, but it is kind of fun. We're going to have to talk but for now I just smiled.

"You know, my mom and I weren't that close. She wasn't a very good wife to my dad. He never complained but I know it hurt him when she left. He gave her everything she wanted, and then when he died, she got the rest. Well, except for the very large part that he left to me."

She looked me in the eye and said, "Very large! He was in oil, not drilling, owning."

My cell phone rang and Chief Dan came on the line.

"Roc, I checked into our serial killer theory and nothing, so far. Looks like this is something new."

"Well, how many similar deaths do you need to classify this as a serial killing?" I asked.

"I guess two."

"Well, maybe we are on to him before he gets too far."

"Yeah, you could be right. We are definitely watching for him now. I've got all the precincts on alert, and they were able to pull some blurry photos from some surveillance cameras downtown. Should be here by the time you arrive."

"Okay, thanks Dan. We'll see you in about 15," and the line went dead.

"Looks like it could be the start of something," I said. "He must be pretty well off if he doesn't rob his victims. Looks like he just toys with them, then smacks them in the head. And the other victim resembled your mom. That's something to focus on. A young surfer guy walking around with his mother. As opposed to me, an old guy walking around with his granddaughter."

She giggled, and I kind of had trouble swallowing. She came to me and kissed me on my thinning head. I didn't notice the lipstick till we got into my car. She giggled some more.

Her phone rang and she talked with one of her girlfriends.

"No. No funeral, cremated. Yeah, well, we can have margaritas on her patio, I guess. Why don't you come down and have dinner with Roc and me this evening? I'll text you the address. Great! We'll see you after while."

She put her phone down.

"That was Margo. You're gonna love her."

"What does that mean?" I asked.

"Oh, she's just very special."

"More special than you?"

"You'll see," she said.

Oh my Lord! I thought.

We looked at the surveillance photos Dan had. Not much to see, really. The crude photographs of who they thought might be the murderer were really blurry but looked a whole lot like the image in my mind. It would probably be too much to ask to get some DNA off the piece of tee shirt they recovered from the floater downtown, so I let it slip from my mind. Dan made us some copies of the killer's picture to show around, and so I wouldn't forget myself; 60, you know.

"You ready for Lunch?" I asked as we drove towards town.

"No, let's hold off. You don't want to spoil your appetite."

"For dinner?".

"For Margo."

I was speechless.

It was about 3:30 when we got back to the complex. There was a new gold color Lexus LS460 parked beside my ol' wreck. I pulled in beside it and out stepped this six foot tall piece of heaven wearing a bright red halter top with a flat tummy straight out of Gold's gym or maybe the best Hollywood surgeon's office, I didn't care which. She had white slacks that could not have been any tighter, high heels of white leather and a handbag that Gucci himself would die for.

"Let me guess, Margo."

"Yep, that's Margo. What do you think?"

"What do I think? I'm not dead, although, I was close this morning."

"Awe, poor baby. Then you might want to have paramedics standing by for tomorrow."

I have to admit, I was a little scared.

Now I'm six foot two and Margo looked me straight in the eyes with her heels on. She came up, hugged me and kissed my forehead and spoke in the absolute sexiest voice I have ever heard, ever.

"Hello Roc."

Ah, Crap! I melted. After a few awkward moments with the two of them looking me up and down and discussing what they saw as if I wasn't there, I broke into the conversation.

"Uh, I need to go to the station and check in with Chief Dan. When I get back we can go to dinner."

I walked out the door, leaving Margo and Pat with beautiful smiles on their gorgeous faces.

"What's up Roc? Didn't expect to see you this afternoon?"

"I want to run something by you."

"Oooh, a Roc theory. I love these."

"I got to thinking, what if these are not random murders?"

"Okay..."

"We know all the women resemble each other; mid sixties, blond, attractive, right?"

"Yeah..."

"What if these murders are just to cover up the real crime?"

"What's the real crime?"

"I'm not sure yet, but what do we know about our victims' financial status?"

"I don't know. Let me do some checking and see what we can shake out of the bushes."

"Thanks, Dan. You'll call me if you find anything?"

"You know I will."

I stopped at the local driving range and hit a large bucket. Not for the practice, but to release some of the tension racking my body and it wasn't from the murders. I was about to escort two beautiful women to dinner and I sure didn't want to appear too eager. It was a quarter to five. I needed to slow things down a bit or this night would last too long. I can be charming for an hour or two at best. After that, I know I'm going to begin looking my age. I figured I would get back to the condo about 6:00, get cleaned up and head to dinner with the ladies about 6:30. Then I could be irresistible for about an hour before the alcohol hits too hard. I can probably stretch this thing 'till about 9:00.

I wasted about thirty five minutes hitting wedges and then I talked to the pro for a while. I ordered a shot but quickly changed that to a cup of joe and an energy drink. I can't start drinking yet. After another cup of coffee I hit the head. What am I doing? There is a reason I don't entertain people. I like my life without the stress and aggravation of trying to keep a relationship. I had just about decided to grab a Crown and a beer and forget this whole night. Then I remembered Margo and the way she looked getting out of her car. Okay. I'll be great just this once. I looked at my watch...5:45. So I made the three-block drive last about fifteen minutes.

I reached the door of my condo, it was unlocked. I stepped in and knew at once there was something different. The curtains were pulled, soft music coming from my speakers, scented candles smelled like apple pie and, clothes strewn across the main room floor. As I turned, I could see that the bedroom door was open and Margo was sitting on the bed. She was under the sheet but somehow I knew she was naked. She had a devious smile on her face. Not a joking or humorous smile, but one that told me what was about to happen. Her hair was beautiful and not one was out of place. There was a distinct glow from behind her, almost as if a Hollywood stage crew had been here to set this whole thing up. She was Beautiful.

"Where's uhh...Pat?" I asked

"She was busy tonight, so she left me in charge."

I was flustered. Thrown off my game and that is not easy to do. I really should have had that drink.

"I guess you don't want to go out to dinner," I said.

"I thought we would stay in tonight."

Hole 4
Laying Up

Pat and Margo came into my room with a large cup of coffee.

"Did we eat dinner last night? I tend to black out sometimes."

"Well, not exactly, but we'll have a nice breakfast for you if you'll get your lazy ass out of bed."

"What time is it?" I asked.

"Going on seven."

"Seven? Uh...I don't usually get up before nine, ladies!"

Well, I guess I'm up now. After a shower, a shave and all the other stuff that goes along with making myself presentable, I tried to remember the last time I had taken my twice daily pills, to no avail. So I loaded a plastic cup with them and threw a couple of extra blood pressure and a few heart pills in the mix. I put on clean, cream colored lightweight linen slacks, the only kind I wear. I buy them on Tuesdays at Goodwilly's

Senior Special, $4 a pair. There are always lots of folks dying to leave their clothes to the Goodwill around San Diego. I added a Tommy Bahama camp shirt and a pair of Steve Madden driving moccasins, no socks. Hey! It's southern California.

If you've never had fresh California berries then you don't know what strawberries taste like. The ladies had waffles with fresh strawberries, fresh squeezed OJ and some baked apples with fresh cream and of course more hot coffee.

My phone rang and JJ was on the other end.

"Hey! You ever gonna play again? I hear through the grapevine that you been slackin' off."

"Not sure you can call what I've been doing slackin' off, but I haven't played since I saw you last week. I got another gig and I need a couple of days to solve a friend's problem. If I live through it I'll give you a call."

"Well, our buddies at the Sporting Club think they have us figured out and want a rematch."

"Don't let them cool off and I'll be with you as soon as I can," I replied.

"You got it, Roc." The line went dead.

Two bites into my waffle and the phone rang again.

"Rocco, its Dan."

"What's up, Pard?"

"I think we got your guy. They're bringing him in as we speak. Can you come by?"

"Yeah, I can be there in about a half hour or so."

"Perfect! I'll see you then."

I told the girls...listen to me! 'The girls.' I sound like the captain of the high school football team talking to a couple of cheerleaders. Let me start over. I told the ladies I had to meet with Chief Dan.

"He has some news on Lisa's killer. I'll be back soon."

I walked out the door with a full stomach, a full mind and a full day ahead. I wondered what, or who would be waiting for me when I got back home. But I had other things to think about right now, so I tried to put that out of my mind. I really need to get back with JJ. I need to golf. My body craves it. Besides, that's how I make a living. I can't get too distracted with other things and let my income slip. I like my life. But still...there was something about this case. I couldn't walk away.

I was standing behind the interrogation window with Dan, listening to one of the detectives question the perp. I was impressed with the way my mind had formulated a picture of this guy, almost down to the length of his blond hair. About an hour and a half later, after he had seen that the cops had photos and the piece of tee shirt, he began to tell his story.

"Thanks for this, Dan."

"Are you kidding? You did all the hard work. I should be thanking you. This guy is a serial killer up and down the coast, and we caught him. This is a big win for our department, and for me. I owe you one, Roc."

"I'm sure I'll collect."

"Anytime my friend, anytime."

I left and drove back home feeling pretty good about the case and how it ended. Who am I kidding? I wasn't happy with the way this situation ended. Sure, we got the guy...or a guy. I couldn't shake the feeling of incompletion. I hate that. I can go out and play nine holes, stop and feel good. I can play eighteen and feel even better. There are only two reasons for me to stop on any other hole. One is 'cause I'm dead. I can't think of any other place I would rather die than while I'm playing golf. The other is when I'm playing for money and the competition concedes before the game is through, in which case I'm actually working and it's okay for me to stop short. But I hate stopping on the seventh, or quitting on the thirteenth. To me, it's like playing Blackjack and only getting dealt one card. It's not done. I need another card, I need another hole, and I need another ending to this case. I can feel it. And therein lies the rub. In life, as in golf your feelings will lie to you. in fact, it is usually a feeling that screws up my golf game. Stick with what you know. Your experience will get you through. Don't over think things. Besides, if there is somebody else involved in this, I'm not sure how to find them. And I'm not sure it would be right to try and convince Pat to keep going. I called Dan back.

"What's up, Roc," he said knowing it was me.

"Dan I just can't shake the idea that we're not done here. Didn't it seem a little too easy? I mean, did he even say why he did it?"

"Some are easy, some are hard. You take the good with the bad, Roc. Besides, we have a full confession and that trumps your feelings every time."

"Well, just let me know if anything weird comes up, will you?"

"You know I will. But hey, don't over think things."

"Yeah, I know. Thanks Dan."

I walked into the clubhouse and found Pat and Margo watching the news on the giant screen.

"How are we doing, ladies?" I asked.

Pat turned and said, "Looks like they got him, right?"

"Looks that way."

"Well, I guess it's time for me to be heading up the coast. There's really not much more I can do here. I hired a realtor to sell the condo and I'll take mom's personal effects with me."

She handed me a manila envelope with a little bulge in one end.

"What's this?" I asked.

"Just a little something for your trouble," she replied.

I opened it and found a check for fifty thousand dollars and the electronic key and title to Lisa's new Bimmer.

"What's this for?" I asked.

"I don't want to go through the trouble to sell it, so you might as well enjoy it."

"And the check?" I asked.

"Compensation for your time. I know I took you away from the course and your livelihood. If that isn't enough, just let me know."

"Are you nuts? That's over ten grand a day," I said.

“It’s my opinion that you my dear, are worth every penny.”

Margo chimed in, “I concur, and maybe more.”

They smiled those big smiles as they walked off.

I sat there watching them leave until they were out of sight and then checked my messages and answered a couple of emails on my cell phone. Then I wandered back to my condo. There was no sign of the ladies. Gone? Yep gone!

I walked over to Lisa’s place and the door was open. The property manager and a couple of maintenance people were already cleaning the unit to get it ready to sell. The lady had walked out of my life just as fast as she had walked in.

“What about all the stuff in here?” I asked.

“Miss May said to let you take anything you want and send the rest to the Goodwill.”

“Goodwill? Everything in here is quality.”

As I looked around for items that I just couldn’t live without I realized that there has to be a hundred grand or more worth of furniture alone, not to mention accessories and appliances. But as much as I wanted some of the things, I just didn’t need them. So I left empty handed. Well, except for the Bimmer. And the steaks I found in the freezer in the garage. And the lobsters that were next to the steaks. And a couple of cases of Crown XO that were next to the freezer. Other than that, I really didn’t need anything.

A week later, I had my buddy from the BMW dealership come out to Lisa’s garage. He had her car loaded onto a flat bed and already had a buyer for it at just under retail. It only had 1800 miles on the odometer. I'm pretty sure she hadn't even had it washed yet. Part of me hated to see it go, but a check for $82,000 in my hand and I was on my way to the bank.

The golf rematch went as expected. They kicked the stakes up a bit. I guess they thought that might throw us off our game. It didn't. You just gotta love rich people. Fifteen thousand! Not bad for a day's work.

I still had over nine thousand in my golf bag from last time and now my bank account was in fine shape, plus another fifty thousand that Pat had blessed me with. Life was pretty good...and then my phone rang.

"Roc. It's Dan."

"Hey Dan. What's up?"

"You're gonna want to hear this. Can you come down to the station?"

"Yeah, sure. I'll be there in about fifteen."

As I pulled up to the station, a car was leaving the spot front and center. I worked up my best Bob Uecker impression.

"I must be in the front row," I said out loud to nobody.

As I made my way back to Chief Dan's Office, I passed the counter that held the coffee maker and half a box of donuts. I poured a Styrofoam cup half way up with coffee and I could already smell the burning. Probably been sitting here for a couple of hours, hence the half cup. I grabbed the last glazed donut and headed back to where I should have been about 10 minutes ago.

"Hey, Roc," Dan said with a huge grin.

"Hey, Dan," I mumbled with a mouthful of what ended up being yesterday's donut.

"Remember last week when Blondie spilled his guts about Lisa's murder?"

"Yeah...?"

"Well, he was lying."

"What? Why?"

Somebody paid him a hundred thousand dollars to take the fall. The money was supposed to be for an operation for his mom. She needed some kind of liver transplant or something."

"Okay...?"

"She died in the hospital this morning."

"So I guess she doesn't need the transplant?"

"Nope. And he doesn't need the money in prison. He cut a deal with the DA."

"So who paid him off?"

"I can only think of one person that has been throwing money around recently," Dan said. "I think she even paid some stupid golfer who ended up pointing us back at her and her friend."

"You mean...?"

"Yup."

"But I thought this guy was a serial killer?"

"Yeah...Would you like to take a guess at who's mother the other victim was?"

"Are you kidding me?" I said in utter disbelief.

"Come on. I'm headed out to pick them up now."

We were in Captain Dan's cop car heading north on the 5 to Capistrano. I really didn't expect to see Pat or Margo again. Funny how things have a way of changing.

Hole 5
Saving Par

Torrey Pines is a fun place, but not near as nice as it looks on TV until a couple of weeks before the big tournament. If you don't know someone, you have to join the lottery. They draw names every day for two weeks down the road. That's BS… I'll quit playing before I'll wait two weeks for a tee time.

We were sitting in the men's grill having breakfast and getting ready for our regular Thursday match when this familiar face came up to me.

"Excuse me, Mr. Reese? Can I have a minute of your time?"

"Do I know you?" I asked.

"Neil, Neil Benson. You watched my dad break his leg in Encinitas?"

It all started to come back.

"Oh yeah, that was funnier than hell!" I said. "So how's your pop Neil?"

"He's dead, Mr. Reese. Someone shot him to death two days ago coming out of his garage."

Sometimes you just put your foot in it and there's nothing you can do except sit there and look really stupid. "Sorry Neil. Sorry for your loss. But how can I possibly help you son?"

"I've heard that sometimes you help people with special problems like this and I was hoping you might look into this for me."

"You've heard wrong, Neil. I'm a golfer, not a cop."

"Please sir. I know that there's something odd here and I could never find out from the police what actually happened, but you could. I would just like a friend that I can trust to take a look."

"Neil, listen..."

"I know you didn't like my dad..."he interrupted.

"I don't think I ever actually said that," I interrupted right back.

"Mr. Reese, please just take a look."

"What do the police have to say about it Neil?"

"They say it was murder and they're investigating, but I'm not sure they're as serious as I would like. Mr. Reese, he wasn't a great man, but he was my dad. I need to know what happened."

"Neil, my day is kind of full. But, if you would like to meet me tomorrow, maybe I could hear you out. Where do you live?"

"Just down the coast a few miles northern part of San Diego."

"Do you know where Jerry's Diner is on PCH?" I asked.

"Yeah. It's just around the corner from my house," Neil said.

Hmmm, nice area. I wondered if there was anything I could really help him with or was I just leading him on.

"How about I meet you there at 9:30 in the morning?" I said.

"Yes, sir. That would be great. I'll see you then." he said and he turned to walked out.

"Neil, I'm not making any promises," I said, probably a little louder than I should have.

"No sir...I mean yes sir, I know. Thank you, Mr. Reese." He hit the door and was gone.

I played like crap. My card read 75 and only won $120. Not even wages. I was thinking about Neil and ol' Ray and wondering how many people in San Diego and all of southern California for that matter, were celebrating because he was dead.

I arrived at Jerry's Diner early, hoping to eat my breakfast alone and just watch Fox News on the flat screen up in the corner. I guess Neil had the same idea. Or maybe he was just anxious. I don't know, but he got there before they had even served my oatmeal. After a few words about the diner, I just started in with the discussion we were here for.

"You know, Neil, your dad wasn't the most amiable person in California?"

"Yeah, I know."

He continued to tell me his theory or theories as it turned out. I ate my oatmeal and 3 cups of coffee. The coffee went right through me so I excused myself right in the middle of Neil's ramblings about why his dad was shot and who might be to blame.

Upon returning to the table, Neil picked the conversation up right where I walked out. I was impressed. It was like he had rehearsed the whole thing and played it back with a pause in the middle, and still never missed a beat.

"My dad was a very successful importer/exporter in southern California. He did a lot of business with China, Korea and Vietnam. He made some enemies over the years because of his brash demeanor, and there have been threats against his life several times."

I listened as Neil told his story until he was done, then I asked a few questions and made some notes on a small pad. My handwriting was getting bad and my spelling wasn't much better. I'm used to score cards. If I can write my name, numbers one to five and draw circles I'm doing great. I try not to need numbers above five and try never to draw a square. I printed everything in my note pad just in case I need to refer back to it later. Or maybe somebody else would need it to figure out what happened to me.

Neil brought up the subject of money.

"How much do you charge Mr. Reese?"

"I don't charge anything, Neil. I'm not a cop or a private investigator. I'm a golfer. But, if you're happy with the results at the end of our relationship, I'll leave it up to you to figure out what you owe me."

"Then you'll do it?" he asked.

"And if I decide that this is going nowhere I reserve the right to just walk away," I said very matter of factly.

He nodded his head in agreement and we shook hands.

I remember one time in between drinks that my father told me, 'There are only two reasons to shake a man's hand: once when you meet him, and again if you trust him.' Few pieces of advice have ever served me better. I always shake hands on a deal. Paperwork is great, but I want people to know where they stand with me. And I always want to be able to look them in the eyes when I shake their hand. You can intimidate people or make them feel comfortable with you, depending on your goal. You can tell so much by a man's handshake. How strong is his grip? How much does he shake up and down? Are his hands sweaty from nervousness? Does he look down or at you? All of these give me a little bit of information about the man I am about to be in a contract with, and you can never have too much information.

"Let's go by your father's home and have a look around?" I said.

As it turned out, Ol' Ray Benson lived just across Interstate 5 from me. It was a very large older home up on the side of a hill, and it was surrounded by lots of Eucalyptus trees and California cactus. It had a big rock garden with benches and a wondering fish pond that encompassed most of the house.

I followed Neil onto the property and we parked to the left of the yellow crime scene tape, at the far end of the six car garage.

As we approached, the garage door in front of us began to open as if on cue, revealing what looked to be a new two tone metallic brown and tan Rolls Royce. Behind that, a Mercedes Gull-Wing coupe in custom English racing green, and behind that a brand new Corvette convertible in midnight black. Just five more rows to go.

I looked at Neil, and he just shrugged, “Yeah, he liked cars.”

“Which one are his golf clubs in?” I asked.

“The Lexus in the first stall. Why?” he asked

“Because that was his regular driver.”

“Yeah...you’re right. Wow, you really do know what your doing.”

“Just common sense, kid.”

I looked at the Lexus. It was an LS 460, a car I knew well and it was metallic red, the same color as mine. I walked up to the crime scene tape and looked over at the chalk outline of a sprawled body on the stamped driveway made to look like cobblestone. I was actually distracted by the driveway. It must have cost a fortune as it ran close to a quarter of a mile down to the main road.

I looked in all directions trying to find what could be the shooter's location.

“Was he coming out or going in when he was shot?” I asked.

“The police say he was coming out of the garage, probably to get the paper.”

“And where was he shot?”

Neil looked at me like I didn’t know what a chalk outline was for.

“What part of his body?” I said.

“In the chest...two days ago...at around 3:30 in the afternoon.”

The only spot that even looked like a possible vantage point was across the 5 in one of the high rise office buildings of downtown San Diego. Wow! What a shot. Definitely not a jealous ex-wife. This was a professional hit.

We walked through the mansion. It hadn't been upgraded in at least forty years. The whole place was antiques, from the kitchen electrical appliances to the hand carved furniture in the library.

"Beautiful! Absolutely beautiful. Neil, can I use the bathroom?"

"Yeah, sure. There's a guest room just down the hall, fourth door on your right."

The so called guest room was as big as my condo. A walk in shower, two walk in closets, separate room for the toilet, walk in room for the basin sink; I couldn't help but open a few cabinet doors. I really wasn't surprised at what I found: pills, pot and powder that I can only assume was coke.

"The old man really took care of his guests," I said out loud but to myself. I looked closer and it was obvious that he didn't have many visitors. I moved a few of the bags and bottles and there was dust marks around each one,

"Oh well! Probably a real party house at one time."

I returned to the living room and once again realized just how big the house was. I passed door after door that I wanted to open, but I knew they would all be just like the one I was just in...empty and dusty.

"Neil, did your dad have any close friends?"

"About the only one I'm aware of is Bob Carlson. They were business partners, and he's probably the only one that could put up with my dad on a regular basis."

"I know that name. From where?" I asked.

"You played golf with him and my dad a few months back."

"Yeah, Yeah. Kind of a quiet guy, late fifties-early sixties, I remember. How was their business relationship?"

"It was great. Dad brought Bob onboard about ten years ago as a partner. He's really good at logistics, took a lot of pressure off my pop."

"What kind of money did they make?"

"Well, Bob probably made two and a half to three million a year, and there's no telling how much my pop took out of the company. Maybe ten or twelve million a year, maybe more."

I whistled.

"Wow! That's some serious bucks. Worth killing for, anyways."

"Mr. Reese, if you're thinking Bob had anything to do with this, you're wrong. Bob Carlson was like a brother to my dad, and like an uncle to me. He would do anything for us. And dad let Bob set his own salary, so it's not the money. Bob would never hurt my pop."

"Well, you've heard of Cain and Able, haven't you?"

"It's not like that. I'm telling you, he wouldn't...."

I could tell this was upsetting him a bit. That's usually when I twist the knife, but Neil was on my side. There was no reason to push him away. Besides, I don't see how this could benefit Bob. No he's partners with Neil, who is a nice guy, but I'm not sure he has the killer instinct that his dad had in business. I tried changing directions.

"Does anyone live here with your dad?" I asked

"Just a full time housekeeper. My mom passed about eight years ago...Cancer."

"Yeah, it took my wife from me. I wouldn't wish that on anyone."

It took about an hour to see all I needed of the mansion. We weren't finished but I was getting tired and had seen all I wanted, at least for now. I was starting to form some interesting thoughts about Ray Benson, and Neil too.

I told Neil that I needed to touch base with my friend, Chief Brown of the SDPD and that I'd be in touch.

I drove to the driving range. I had in mind hitting a bucket but by the time I got there I just walked straight into the bar, sat down with a couple of buddies and ordered a Crown on the rocks. Actually I didn't order it. Brady, the bartender saw me coming through the door and had it ready. He handed it to me as I got to the table.

"Missed you today, Roc," one of my buddies said.

"Yeah, got an acquaintance that needs some help and I couldn't find a way to turn him down."

I had a couple more cocktails and then decided I better call Chief Dan before he started drinking for the evening.

"Dan, it's Roc. I need to pick your mind for a minute or two. Want to meet me at Jaxons? I'll buy dinner."

"Best offer I've had to date. See you in 30," he said.

I had just taken my first sip of Crown when Dan walked in.

"Hey Roc! What's on your mind?"

He sat at the bar beside me and before I could answer my favorite waitress walked up.

"Hey Lucy, my regular and a slice of you if ya don't mind," he said.

"Sorry Chief, you're next in line behind Roc, and I got a feeling he's not gonna be giving up his spot," she answered without skipping a beat.

"Lord, if only she wasn't just kidding," I said.

"I'm not sure she is," Dan said.

"My granddaughter is older than her," I replied.

"Yeah, but she's not your granddaughter."

We ordered fried shrimp with chips and a salad and as usual it was perfect.

"So what's so important you're willing to spend a quarter for my dinner?" Dan asked.

"You've got a murder case, Ray Benson. Millionaire-businessman who was whacked in his driveway a couple of days ago."

"Yeah, Yeah! Still gathering evidence on that one."

"Have you been to the scene?" I asked.

"Yeah, I was there right after the shooting, Why?"

"Have you got anything yet?"

"No...kind of strange. Can't seem to put this one together. Why? You know the guy?"

"Not really, but looks to me like a pro job, from one of those skyscrapers across the five."

Dan looked me in the eye.

"Do you know how far that is?" He asked.

"Yeah, 'bout 3/4 of a mile, best I can tell. That's why I said, a pro job."

"More than a pro. More like a world class sniper," Dan said. I could see the wheels start to turn.

"This is starting to sound less and less like a jealous husband and more like a pissed off foreign government."

"Yeah. Hey, what time did you guys estimate this all happened?" I asked as I took another bite of perfectly fried shrimp.

"Lividity puts the time of death between two and four in the afternoon. Why? What are you thinking?"

"Just gathering info. Man, I should have been a cop."

"Uh...I don't think so."

"Why not...you don't think I could do it?"

"Roc, you're an amazing golfer and a great detective, but you'd be a terrible cop!"

"Yeah, you're right. Besides, you'd have to explain why you're paying me a couple hundred grand a year to play golf every day."

"Yeah, and this way I get you for free."

"Hey, wait a minute," and we both smiled.

"And dinner to boot," I said.

We ate and drank and kept an eye on the gorgeous help and all in all, life was pretty good.

Hole 6
From the Tips

The next morning about ten, I was in the parking lot of B&C Enterprises; Benson and Carlson I'm assuming. I guess I'd find out soon enough. I took the elevator up to the 22nd floor; the corporate offices. As it turned out my assumption was spot on. Bob Carlson walked out of what can only be described as a humungous office and shook my hand.

"Come on in Mr. Reese, have a seat."

"Please, just call me Roc. Wow, what a view!"

"Yeah, it is pretty spectacular, isn't it?"

"That's an understatement," I said.

To the southwest, the Pacific Ocean and southeast, a perfect view of the hill that Neil's pop had settled on for the last forty plus years. I walked over to my left up to a huge sliding window perfectly framing Ray's house. I tried to squint to see if I could make out any detail up Rays driveway.

"Can you see your casa from here Bob? You don't mind me calling you Bob, I hope?"

"Not at all, Roc. See that mansion up near the top of the mountain?" Bob said pointing to Ray's house.

"Yeah. Wow! What a spread, is that yours?"

"No, No. That's Ray's. The one to the left of that about half way down the hill, that's me."

"Well, I'm so sorry," I said sarcastically. "What is that, about 100,000 square feet?"

"Nah, only 21,000," he replied like he was stuck in a room at the YMCA.

"Ray's place is the monster, 67,000 square feet. Indoor pool, outdoor pool, bowling alley and as far as I know he never rolled a ball in his life."

"Wow!"

"Yeah, and a twenty seat movie theater with a popcorn machine, a slot car track and a whole bunch of whistles and bells I can't think of at the moment."

"Wow, and he could just sit at his desk and keep an eye on it. How far do you think it might be from here, as the crow flies?"

"Oh, I don't know, probably a mile or more I suppose!"

"Yeah, that's the figure I was thinking myself," I lied.

I have found over the years that it is always better to agree with a man in his office. Being on another man's turf is a shaky thing. He has the advantage. When I get people in neutral territory, then I can play a little harder. That is why I always try to meet at a restaurant or on the course. Besides, I didn't want to show any face cards yet. I wasn't exactly sure who I could trust.

"Mind if we take a look in Ray's office," I asked.

"Of course, follow me. His is identical to mine, except it faces north and the decor is a little different style is all."

Bob's was modern to the max, but Ray's was antique golf from the floor up; old wooden shafted clubs everywhere, original paintings of Augusta National, Torrey Pines, Pebble Beach and many more. I recognized every one. I wasn't sure about the artists but they all appeared to be museum quality.

"Wow, great paintings," I said trying to sound more interested in the decor than the reason I was here. To be honest, I was. These really were great paintings. Half a dozen hole in one trophy's and all of a sudden I lost my interest. I played a round with Ray, well, sixteen holes anyway, and I doubt if one of those were his, unless he bounced it off a golf cart, maybe. I looked around the office and it had the exact opposite view as Bob's. Pacific on my left, mountain on my right, it was the same office; right down to the big four by eight foot sliding glass window that faced the mountain of death. The only difference was this window frame had scratches on it; the kind that might be made by a rifle when it recoils. I looked around the room but nothing jumped out at me.

"Thanks for the tour, and holler at me if you want to go swing a stick again."

I shook hands with Bob and headed back down to the parking lot. It didn't seem to surprise him that I was nosing around. Maybe Neil had told him he was hiring me. Or maybe...oh, I don't know.

I met Dan at Jaxon's for cocktails and some oysters on the half shell. The food was good and the conversation was fine. Small talk mainly, nothing new in the case on his end. But the real reason I was here...I just wanted another look at Lucy. And then...

"Hey Big fella, you stood me up last night," she said with a pout on her pretty face.

I looked around to see who she was talking to. Dan had just left and I was the only one in the bar at the moment.

"You talkin' to me?" I said with my best De Niro impression as I looked around the bar. Yep! We were alone.

"Yeah! I'm talkin' to you. I thought we had a date."

"I think your confusing me with a younger guy."

She stopped and pretended to be in deep thought for a second and then replied, "Nope. It's you."

"Why?" I asked.

"Why not? You're a good looking guy and you make me laugh." You want another chance?" she asked.

"You're not pulling my leg are you?"

"Of course not, Roc. Why would I?"

"What time do you get off?" I asked.

"Same time as last night, Six."

"Uh...okay, how about supper? You do feed the beautiful body occasionally, don't ya?"

"Yeah! At least twice everyday."

"Well, okay then. Let me run home and shower and I'll pick you up at six. Uh, where?"

"Don't worry about it. I'll swing by your condo, that way I won't get stood up again."

"You know where I live?"

"Yeah, my dad lives there too."

"Great!?! He's not one of them shotgun daddy's, is he?"

"Don't worry love. He eats at 4:30 and he's asleep in his recliner by six."

I know that feeling I thought to myself.

"I guess I don't need to tell you what number then do I?"

"Nope, I'm good."

"You sure are," and I walked out leaving cash for my tab and a twenty dollar tip on the bar.

Lucy showed at ten after six. I had already begun thinking that it was a practical joke. I wasn't amused.

"Mind if I grab a quick shower, love?"

She was already out of her denim cut-offs and her tank top sailed thru the air and landed on the floor by the bed. Oh crap! I couldn't see but, I knew she was one of those So Cal phenoms that looked even better with her clothes off.

I don't slice. A slice in golf is caused by one of two things: a problem with your swing or a problem in your head. My swing is smooth every time. I know it and I trust it. No matter the situation, I know my swing is right. And I am not easily jarred under pressure. Raise the stakes and I thrive. I love it. But...there are different kinds of pressure, and this is a new one. I wasn't sure why, but I really didn't want to screw this up.

"Lucy girl! What do you drink?" I hollered through the bathroom door.

"Anything on the rocks, Roc!"

I heard her giggle and it made me smile. I had been trying to understand what this was all about for the last two hours and all I have been able to come up with is that she must be tied in with ol' Ray's killer. Her job is to get rid of me, Death by sex!

"Ah hell, this has got to be one of the best ways to go, ever."

I threw my California ID on the bed stand just in case she needed some more info on me and headed to the patio with our drinks. She was coming out of the bathroom as I was opening the sliding patio door and her bath towel fell to the floor.

"Oh! Roc? Hi!" and she scooped it up and stepped into my bedroom. I just smiled

I was sitting on the patio watching the sunset when she came out wearing one of my old white dress shirts. She picked up her drink and backed up against the railing and I swear my heart stopped. She was standing between me and the setting sun and the view was magnificent.

"This tastes so good, Roc. What did you do to it?"

"I let my finger soak in it for a minute, 'cause I'm so sweet, don't cha know?"

"You truly are!" She bent forward and kissed me on the forehead. "It just doesn't get any better than the California coast sunsets, does it Roc?"

"No, this is about the best view I believe I have ever seen," I said still looking at her silhouette.

She giggled and came to sit in the other chair beside the small glass table.

"Roc! Would you mind if we ate in tonight? I'll buy."

"I don't mind at all, and I think I can afford to pay for dinner. What's your pleasure?" I asked.

"I know this really good place just around the corner and they deliver. Your regular, Roc?"

"Yeah! Why not?"

I heard Lucy say hi to the night bartender and order two shrimp dinners with salad.

"Yeah, blue cheese. Yeah, number 18."

She walked back out to the patio and we drank and watched the sunset, I had a bottle of wine in the icebox from when Pat and Margo were here.

"Does this stuff go bad?" I asked Lucy.

"Have you kept it in a bottle?" She asked.

"Yeah!"

"It's white wine. It should be fine."

The doorbell rang. I smiled and handed her two glasses and the large bottle, and I went to answer it. We dined on fried shrimp, crispy truffle fries and a fresh garden salad with Roquefort and some Kings Hawaiian rolls. Life was good, kind of scary but very good. We sat on the patio and listened to the surf pound the sand and sipped Crown Royal 'till around ten. Without saying a word, Lucy got up, changed back into her cut offs and tank top and left.

What just happened? I guess it was too good to be true. I had a couple more Crowns, this time without the rocks and headed off to bed. It took me a little longer than usual to get to sleep. I guess I still had that vision of Lucy in my shirt, backed up against the patio rail in the sunset, on my mind. Maybe she's just a very lonely, very nice girl...with the most incredible body ever.

Hole 7
Slice

I had just come back from a two mile kayak ride up the coast and was sitting on the patio with a hot cup of joe when the doorbell rang. What's that little guy's name with the wings on his heels that delivers flowers? Well, anyway, he was at my door with a bouquet of roses. He looked me over from head to toe and started to smile.

"You got something to say squirt?" And the smile disappeared.

"Uh, No sir. Uh..."he looked at the name on the card.

"Mr. Reese? Uh, these are for you, sir."

"No, Mr. Reese is my father. He's still asleep."

He turned red. I reached in the pocket of my shorts and pulled out a fiver. Crap! I was hoping it would be a receipt from Wal-Mart so I could stiff him.

"Thanks Mr. Reese," and he was off, like he had wings on his...well, you know. The card read...

"Roc, Sorry about last night. You obviously weren't interested and I didn't mean to push. If you ever are interested, I would love to see you again. If not, I understand. With love, Lucy."

My cell phone rang about 8:30 as I drove up PCH and I didn't even hear it.

"Not interested? Are you nuts lady?" I said out loud. I had a real hard time keeping my mind on Neil's case or golf or driving. I almost caused three accidents and Chief Dan was a witness to the last one. I pulled into McDonalds and ordered two senior coffees and sat at one of those really tight little plastic booths that they're so proud of and waited for Chief Dan to sit down.

"Where's your PJ's, Roc? You're driving like you're asleep."

"Really funny, Dan!"

"What's going on with you this morning?"

"Lucy!" I replied.

"You mean the bartender, Lucy? That Lucy?"

"Yeah! That Lucy."

"Did you hit that last night?"

"No! But I'm in big trouble because I didn't."

"Well, that's a special kind of trouble to have. Wanna talk about it?" he smiled.

"No. I don't. Did you check out Bob Carlson?" I asked.

"I did, and there's nothing to suggest he could hit a barn with a shotgun from ten yards. He did four years in the Navy behind a desk, that's where he learned his trade."

"Well, someone had access to Ray's office and it looks like the shot came from the sliding window.

There's scratch marks that suggest it. What about Neil? Anything on him I should know about? I don't want to give anything away if he's a suspect."

"Nah! We've checked him out and he's squeaky clean, so far. Not a sportsman or an outdoors man of any sort. I think he could lift a house, but I don't see him shooting anyone and it looks like he truly cared about his dad."

"I'm gonna meet with him this morning and I'm still very concerned about how someone could get up to Ray's office in the middle of the day without being detected, unless they were supposed to be there, like maintenance or cleaning staff. Dan, maybe you should check and see if they had any food catered on that day."

"Good idea, Roc, I guess I should be buying the coffee."

"Don't worry about it Dan. When your income matches mine, you can buy anything you want."

We parted and I was off to keep my meeting with young Neil.

On the way I decided to see if my Bluetooth was working. It was almost eleven and Jaxon's was open for lunch, so I called. A very friendly and familiar voice filled my whole car.

"Good morning, Jaxon's, May I help you?"

"You sent me red roses. Every woman in San Diego under the age of forty knows I like yellow!"

Lucy giggled that little laugh that I was getting so used to.

"I'm so sorry! I guess I haven't been ignored often enough yet to know all your special little idiosyncrasies."

"Hey, I'm so sorry. I thought I was being a gentleman. I didn't realize you wanted to move so fast."

"If I wanted a gentleman, I'd go out with Mr. Jaxon."

This time I giggled.

"Would you like to give it one more shot, or should we just walk away?" I asked.

"I absolutely would like to give it one more shot and I promise no more flowers. I get off at four today."

"Give me your address and I'll pick you up at six, and this time we're going out for dinner!"

"Yes sir, Mr. Reese." I'll text it to you when I get caught up here."

"Oh, I don't do that texting thing," I said.

"Have one of the nurses at the home explain it to you. I gotta go."

"What did she just say to me? At the home?" I questioned myself out loud, and my Bluetooth made a sound like a dial tone all over the inside of my car.

I met with Neil and told him what I had found. Well, most of it anyway. I told him we were narrowing the possibilities and that I'd stay in touch.

At ten 'til six I was standing outside Lucy's very exclusive apartment building, just about to ring her security bell when the door buzzed. I opened it and walked into a really nice foyer and made my way over to the elevator. My last date was with Pat and Margo over three months ago and I swore I would never see the likes of those two again in my lifetime. Man, was I wrong.

Lucy opened the door, and the most beautiful creature on the face of my Lords earth stood before me. She had a white knit skirt hemmed a few inches above the knee, a matching halter top, a natural turquoise necklace and matching color heels. Her long blond hair that I had only seen in a ponytail hung over both shoulders almost to her breast, but not quite. Her abs were exposed and defined and they would put Mayweather to shame. I did a double take and realized that she wasn't wearing a bra. Perfect form without a bra...unbelievable.

"Would you like to come in for a drink?" she asked.

"Hell no! I want to go to every night spot in town and show off my date just home from college."

She giggled, and we were gone. We had cocktails at a couple of the high-rise restaurants overlooking the ocean and everywhere we went she turned heads; young men, old men, gay men, and even some women. Yeah, she was that hot and I was escorting her. I know some of the head turning was about her being with the likes of me, and I loved it. It's not often that a guy like me gets arm candy, and I was going to enjoy every minute of it.

We ended up having dinner at the most exclusive restaurant on the coast of California in La Jolla. We had a private dining room just above the caves. They had spot lights on the water with a glass barrier to keep the cool ocean air away from us and a butane heater in the corner, just warm enough to keep us comfortable. We could hear the Sea lions serenading us and it was a truly magical evening, so far.

"Roc, this is just the most perfect evening ever. I didn't even know this place was here."

"I had forgotten it was here. It was a favorite of Jennie's. I haven't been here since she passed away."

"Probably just as well. From the lack of prices on the menu, I don't think I make enough in a month to afford to eat here."

We finished our meal and the tab with the tip was right at $800, and worth every penny...uh dollar. Good thing I had gone to my golf bag for some cash earlier in the day. Places like this love cash.

On our way back down the coast she was looking around the inside of my car. She opened the glove compartment, pulled down the visors and even tried to look behind the seats. I wasn't exactly sure what she was doing and normally I would put a stop to anyone taking that initiative with my car, but for some reason, Lucy looking around didn't seem to bother me at all.

"If you're looking for me, I'm over here," I stated.

"Roc! What year is this car? It looks brand new."

"It's an '08, but I try to keep it up. They're pretty hard to wear out if you take care of them."

"I'm in the market for something new, or at least newish. Would you consider helping me find a good used one?"

"Sure! How much money do you have to spend?" I asked.

"Well! I don't want any payments, so I guess about 25 or 26."

"When it comes to finding deals you're talking to the master. Lots of old people dying to get rid of their cars in the area."

She put her lovely manicured hand on my thigh as we pulled back into the north end of town.

"Your place or mine?"

"WOW!"

"Was that too forward for you?"

"No! Not at all. It's just that I'm with the most beautiful woman in the entire world and she wants to take me home. I feel like I'm dreaming."

"I'm not sure I've ever been somebody's dream before."

"Yes you have, Doll. I can assure you, you have."

"Well, I'll try and make your dreams come true. Turn here and I'll show you my place," she said.

Lucy, as it turns out had a degree in interior design. After a fresh cocktail I got the grand tour and for an 1100 sq ft. apartment it was remarkable, very eclectic, but everything worked perfectly.

"Do you have any photos of this place?" I asked.

"Yeah, I do. I've sent them off to several magazines but never heard back from any of them.

"Let me make a few calls. Jeanie was very well connected in the design business."

"Wow, Roc. That would be great. Thanks."

"Well, no promises."

I was looking at some of the artwork on the walls and taking a pull on my Crown on the rocks as I turned back to face Lucy when I almost choked. She was standing in front of me with nothing on but her high heels and a pearl necklace.

"Time for that dream we were talking about," she said in a soft beautiful voice. She slowly walked over to me, took my glass out of my hand and placed it on the end table next to us. Without missing a step, she reached up and placed her hand behind my neck and pulled me down into a kiss.

"Even better than my dream," I said as we made our way to the bedroom.

The next morning she had fresh squeezed orange juice, Eggs Benedict, fresh strawberries in cream and some of the best coffee I have ever tasted. We made small talk for a while, then I stood to leave and she glared at me with that pouty look.

"What?" I asked.

"Don't you want to see me again?" she asked.

"Of course, but I thought I would play it cool and call you later today."

"Well, I'd rather know right now."

"Well, I would love to see you, right now."

She stood and dropped her robe.

"Okay! Okay! I surrender. But just how is this going to end?" I asked.

"Why does it have to end? Why can't we be friends with benefits? I go out with other people, but you'll be first on the list if you want," she said.

"Wow! That's a great offer. Really. But Lucy, I'm not that guy. I like you and I really like being with you, but I've never really seen myself as one of the options. I'm better than that. I'm not asking for a commitment or anything. Just, when you need to move on, let me know. Till then, you're either with me or you're not. We can always be friends."

She didn't even flinch, almost like she didn't hear me.

"I'll see you at your place about six? I love the view and I'll cook."

"I'll see you tonight, Beautiful."

I wasn't sure if we had an agreement or not. I wasn't sure I cared. I guess I would find out soon enough. This was a young man's game and I was still in it, for now.

I made a couple of calls as I drove; one to my friend at the BMW dealership in La Jolla and one to the old lady that was in charge of the Southern California Interior Design Society. I asked her to take a look at Lucy's web page and she assured me she would. I smiled knowing that Lucy would be happy about that.

Hole 8
Pitch and Run

My phone rang.

"Roc! It's JJ, you okay?"

"JJ! You wouldn't believe me if I told you. What's up?"

"Meet me for a bowl of chowder. I got a couple of things I want to run by you," he said.

"You got it. I'm about five minutes out."

Chowder only meant one place in the middle of the day; our favorite spot on the beach on Andy Devine Boulevard in Del Mar. I pulled into the parking lot and checked my mirror and JJ's Jag was pulling in right behind me. A medium bowl of chowder and a ice cold beer and life was good, for a minute.

"What's on your mind, JJ? Must be pretty important to get you off the course on a Thursday."

"I was at Torrey last night and I overheard a couple of Mexican Mafia types talking. Your name came up."

"Really? In what way?" I asked.

"We were sitting at the bar and I sure didn't want to make it too obvious that I was trying to listen, but it sounded like there was a hit on you and they were planning their attack."

"Why would anyone want to kill a harmless ol' fart like me?"

"Well, you are old and you do fart a lot but you're certainly not harmless and it sounds like you may have your nose in someone else's business."

I was leaning forward taking a spoon full of the best chowder on the coast, and I knew something was wrong. Time slowed for a moment and I was thinking very fast. Had I hit a nerve with someone? How dangerous could this be? There are times when I am on the course setting up for a shot and I just know the ball is going into the hole. It doesn't happen often, but on occasion, I just get that feeling that this shot will be the perfect shot, and sure enough, in the hole. That is exactly how I was feeling right now. It may be the first time I've felt it when I wasn't on the course. But what does it mean now? I leaned back in my chair to think about it when my bowl exploded and soup flew every where. Without thinking I knew exactly what had just happened. Instinct took over and I spun around and intentionally fell sideways onto the floor, grabbing JJ's arm and pulling him down with me. The bullet hit the cement and then tore apart the right ankle of the lady sitting at the table next to us. Blood began squirting everywhere.

"Get down," I hollered as loud a I could.

Turning, I saw a vehicle up on PCH spin out leaving sand and gravel flying everywhere. It was a late model Ford Explorer or Expedition with blacked out windows; against the law in California. I grabbed my phone and hit #3 and Chief Dan came on the line.

"Hey Rocco! What's on your mind?"

"JJ and me are at the San Castle having lunch and someone tried to punch my ticket! High powered rifle. Big black Ford SUV headed south with blacked out windows; shouldn't be too hard to find. But we need an ambulance along with the cops; a lady next to me just about lost her foot.

"They're on the way! Shouldn't be more than a couple of minutes. Are you okay, Roc?"

"Well, I don't know. How do you get clam chowder out of...Hey JJ, what kind of material is this shirt?"

"Yeah, you're fine. I'm on my way," Dan said and the line went dead.

The fire station was just across the bridge north of the bay from the race track. I heard the siren start to scream as I hung up. I learned to water ski in this particular bay when I was in junior high; my grandparents lived in the area. I guess that had something to do with why I settled around here; water, weather, waitresses, and bikinis. That doesn't start with W, but it definitely needs to be included.

I grabbed as many cloth napkins off the nearby tables as I could and made a compress on the lady's leg. I started yelling at the top of my lungs not to panic, trying to let everybody know that the shooter is gone, but by the time I got to the middle of my sentence I realized that nobody was listening. My yelling turned into talking which turned into talking to myself. People were pushing and shoving in a panic; a frantic mass. They would have made a perfect target if the shooter was still around.

JJ and I tried to pay our bill but Reagan, the manager wouldn't take our money. We tried to get away before the TV news showed up but no luck. They met us between the front door and the parking lot.

"Sorry! You'll have to ask the police," I told several reporters and I made my way to my car. I looked over at JJ.

"You need to stay away from me for a few days. If I don't make our tee time next Wednesday, you'll know they got me," I smiled.

"Hey! That's not funny," he said.

"I know. It really isn't, but it kind of is. I've had a pretty good life. In fact, after last night I don't know how it could get any better."

"Just keep your head down!"

"I will," I assured him and punched the big V-8 and laid a strip of rubber down the PCH, then dropped it into second and left another strip. I was still kind of hungry, and now very angry. If I went home now, I might end up talking about this whole mess, and I did not want to talk about it. I hit a bucket of balls and putted for an hour or so and then checked my watch. It was about ten till six. I threw my wedges and putter in the trunk and left the driving range heading home; this time with great anticipation.

"How did you get in?" I asked.

"With a key of course!" Lucy said with a smirk.

"Where did you get a key?"

"Under the cute little cherub in the rocks by the rose bush. If you were a key, where would you be?"

"Is nothing sacred any more?"

"All I know is for a detective; you're not very good at hiding things."

"I'm not a detective," I replied. "I'm a golfer."

"Whatever. Why don't you grab a shower and I'll start dinner."

"I was about half way through my shower when I felt arms around my waist.

"Who's there?" I asked.

"Very funny."

Dinner was amazing. We ate Filet Mignon charred medium then finished off in Black Truffle oil with sautéed mushrooms, grilled asparagus and some romaine hearts with homemade blue cheese dressing. We had a very good red wine that I couldn't pronounce and then some fresh strawberries to dunk in whipped cream. We finished with a very smooth Brandy and then some more Crown as we watched the moon reflect off the water.

I woke alone in my California King Tempur Pedic and thought I pissed her off again. Then, I heard her voice and I was sure of it.

"Rockland Reese!"

Uh ohh, my full name. This can't be good. I remember getting in trouble when I was a kid and my mom would call me by my full name, but she would use my middle name too. There is just something about using a middle name that just instills fear. Every time I heard it, I would instantly go through my last twelve to twenty four hours of life and try and figure out what I was about to be beaten for. Did I forget to take out the trash? Did I miss the toilet again? Did I superglue my sister's favorite doll to the cat? At least Lucy didn't know my middle name...I think.

"Yes dear?" I said, half with sarcasm.

"Did you have anything you wanted to tell me about yesterday?" she inquired as she walked back into the room.

"Umm...oh yeah, I stopped off at the driving range for a while. Sorry. It completely slipped my mind."

"This isn't funny. Why didn't you tell me you were almost killed?"

"Oh, that! It's not what you think."

"I think you were almost killed," she half-screamed.

"It really wasn't that bad. Hey, you want to go look at some cars today?" I asked trying to change the subject.

"Cars? Are you crazy?"

"Are you talking to me?"

"Yeah! Who the hell else did I sleep with last night?"

"Speaking of sleeping, are we ok?" I redirected.

"Yeah, we're great. We snuggled all night. I guess we both needed a good night's rest...and don't change the subject," she began yelling again as she left the room.

"No, of course not. Hey, your hair looks really pretty this morning. Did you do something different?"

"I'm not joking, Roc. We are going to talk about this."

"Yes, of course we are. Hey, do we have any coff...?"

Before I could finish my sentence, she walked back in with two cups of coffee and her...uhh my shirt hanging wide open.

"Can we talk about the way you walk around here?"

"You don't like the way I walk?" she pouted.

"No, no, I mean the way you dress!"

"So now you don't like the way I dress, either?"

"No! That's not what I meant. I love the way you dress. It's just that I'm about to have a heart attack and I don't have any insurance. I'm not sure I'm healthy enough for this everyday."

"Then we will have to get you exercising."

She handed me a cup of really good coffee and joined me in bed.

"What time is it?" I asked.

"5:30. Why?"

"In the morning?" I shouted. "What the hell are we doing awake before dawn?"

"Well, I guess we can start your exercise program. Come here."

The next time I looked it was 9:47 and I felt considerably better.

"I hope this relationship is working for you 'cause it's doing wonders for me," I said bending over and kissing her belly button and then I headed for the shower.

Cream colored linen slacks, my saddle colored driving moccasins and a Tommy Bahama Camp shirt with a tail long enough to cover my Glock; and I was ready for the day.

“Do you always carry that?” she pointed at my pistol.

“Let’s just say it’s always with me. Does it bother you?”

“No, not at all. In fact, I’ve been thinking of taking the Concealed Carry course myself. It’s getting crazy out there. How long have you carried?”

“Ever since I got out of the service, about forty years ago. I carry large amounts of cash from time to time and it just makes good sense to be protected. You really should take the course. You want to go look at some cars?”

“Are we gonna get shot while we do?” she asked with a smile.

“No guarantees,” I replied. “But wouldn’t you rather die in a new car?”

“I’d rather not die!”

“Noted. Hey, let me ask you a serious question. Do you need someone to paint those jeans on every day?”

“Are you volunteering my darling?”

“Yeah! I guess I am.”

She slipped into a tank top that could have been skin if it hadn’t been green. There just wasn’t a flaw anywhere...for the moment.

Hole 9
Roll It and Hole It

We met my friend in La Jolla at the Bimmer dealership and looked at several pre owned luxury cars. Nothing really blew her dress up, so to speak. As we were walking off the lot a service man drove a BMW sports model and parked it by the street.

"Roc, look at that! That's the one."

"What is that?" I asked my friend.

"Oh, that just came from an estate sale. It's a 2008 M6 X with 31K and it's like new."

"How much?" she asked.

"I could let it go for around 28," he said.

Lucy put that beautiful pouty face look in his direction, and he began to smile out of one side of his mouth while he tried to look away.

"You want me to see what I can do?" I whispered.

"I got this," she said. Forty five minutes later we left the lot.

"Let's drop your car off and we'll blow the dust out of this thing," she said with a smile. She met me and we took off towards the San Bernardino Mountains, hit the 10 and she could drive too.

"How much did you give for this?" I asked.

"25 and some change, but I would have gone a lot higher. I guess he liked me."

"Go figure!" I said.

The next morning sitting in the lodge in Big Bear eating flapjacks and eggs, we tried to decide what to do about the shooters that were determined to snuff me out. Lucy was truly concerned about me. I was trying to act like I didn't take it too seriously, but I did and I think she knew it. She tossed me the keys and we came down the mountain a little faster than she was used to. I hit the 10 back into LA, then the 5 and headed south to San Diego.

I talked to Dan and asked if he had any leads on the shooter. He said he thought that it was probably the same guy who shot Ray Benson.

"The guy that shot at me wasn't the same guy that shot Ray or I'd be walking around dead right now. Unless...."

"Unless what?"

"...Unless they were just trying to scare me off."

"Good thought," Dan said. Let me do some more digging and I'll get back to you."

"Thanks Chief," I said and hung up.

"Is there anyone in Southern California that's not on your friends list?" Lucy asked.

"Well, I can think of one guy out there right now." I put my hand on her very firm thigh and she picked it up and kissed it. Damn! I wished I knew what her angle was, but I really don't want to know.

I put channel 19 on her Sirius radio and surprisingly enough she took a liking to Elvis right off.

"But I can't help falling in love with you."

Then I turned on channel 5, the 50s, and found the Fat man singing Blueberry Hill.

"Don't push it buster!" Lucy said and I turned back to Elvis.

I couldn't find a single thing wrong with the Bimmer; at 60, at 80, even at 110; and it averaged 27 mpg at high speed. It was every bit as quick as my 460, maybe even a little quicker and more responsive.

I got off the 5 and headed into La Jolla and then south on the PCH. We were downtown La Jolla when I spotted the big black Ford SUV in the rear view.

"Lucy, you'd better tighten your seat belt."

"What is it?" she said with concern in her voice.

"Look's like the same SUV I saw the other day."

I dropped her Bimmer down into manual and went threw the township in low gear. As soon as we reached the south end of town I punched it. Tires squealed and we were off. Unfortunately, the traffic on the PCH was enough to keep me from getting very far ahead and just as we passed the BMW dealership the SUV hit us hard from the rear. They swerved hard to the left and came up on my side of the car. The blacked out passenger window lowered and an automatic assault rifle came in view. I slammed my foot down on the break just as a dozen or more bullet holes appeared across the hood of Lucy's new car.

"Sorry, Love," I said as I pulled my Glock 26 from my holster on my waist and slammed a 9mm round home into the chamber.

"Just get us out of here," she yelled.

Lucy had a hold of the hand grip just above the door and her knuckles were turning white and some of the perfect tan on her face had started to fade as well. I jammed the throttle to the floor and we flew by the SUV on the right.

They pulled in behind us, and we were in and out of traffic. Just then the shooter let another burst loose that blew the back window out. The rounds passed right between Lucy and me going on through the windshield and it was riddled with holes and cracks.

"You'd better get your head down and keep it there."

She bent over to her left and put her head in my lap.

"Really Love, now?"

I'm not sure she got the humor, and it really wasn't the right time to discuss it. The big SUV pulled even with us on my side again and it looked like we were sitting ducks. Cars ahead in both lanes, cars parked along the PCH and a city cop had joined the fun and was about ten car lengths back. Just as the window on the passenger's side started to lower, I decided it was my turn.

I rested the Glock on my left arm and put a round in the right ear of the passenger and he slumped forward. I immediately aimed to hit the driver in his right arm in hopes of slowing him down so the cops could take over, but I hit a small pothole entering an intersection just as I squeezed the trigger. The 9mm bullet hit him just above his right ear and I knew he was gone. The big black Ford swerved hard to the right, against the driver's side of the Bimmer grinding off paint and putting big gouges from the front all the way to the back. Then it forced me up against the row of very expensive cars parked along the PCH, peeling the front quarter panel off Lucy's car like it was a layer of California lettuce. Lucy's door panel came off and slid under the rapidly deteriorating Bimmer, and the rear quarter panel on her side crumbled. I had pretty much the same results happening on my side. All of a sudden, I lost what little control of the vehicle I had. With both feet pushing on the brake pedal, I could feel the front wheels collapse and buckle under as the frame started to bend and we slid across the street and hit a fire hydrant, dead on the BMW logo. We came to rest, teetering on the sheared off hydrant with several thousand pounds of water pressure being forced up through the floorboard and into the cabin of Lucy's new car. The SUV had us pinned in on my side and the front of a new Cadillac that was illegally parked on the side street had us trapped on Lucy's side. I already had pushed the button for Chief Dan by the time we had come to a stop.

"Dan, have you been watching the chase down the PCH?"

"The Bimmer sportster and the Ford SUV? Yeah! Are you in the area?"

"You could say that! Watch your screen, I'll wave to you."

"Holy crap, Roc! Is that you on the water spout.

"Yep, me... and the alluring Miss Lucy. Just out for a Sunday drive in her brand new Bimmer. Got a city cop behind us but I could really use your help. I had to whack a couple of shooters that pulled an automatic on me. I'm not sure this city cop is going to understand my position in what is going on here."

"I'm not sure I understand your position in what is going on here," Dan said.

"Dan..."

"My guys are just around the corner, Roc. Need the paramedics?"

"No, we're okay, but if you would call the Bimmer dealership across the street and have the manager walk over, that would help."

"You got it Roc."

I looked at Lucy and the color was returning to her face.

"How you doing, Girl?"

"Well, let's just say I have never been so happy in my life to have taken out insurance."

"What's that all about?" I asked.

"I paid two hundred dollars for a temporary policy worth thirty thousand while I got my insurance company set up. It's good for 2 weeks."

"Smart girl. I guess we should go look at cars when they cut us loose here."

"I guess," she agreed.

Water was up to our chest and pouring out the open windows in back. Lucy looked beautiful. I couldn't believe it. After everything we just went through, she still looks great. There is definitely something about her.

Dan, the press, tourists and just about any one that was anyone in the greater San Diego area was standing around the sidewalks.

"You're getting to be quite the TV personality lately," Dan said.

"Yeah, and quite the target as well," said Lucy.

"Well, I'm not trying to be either."

JJ drove by headed north on PCH. He honked and shouted out the window.

"You need a ride, Roc?"

I just waved. I watched him smile, shake his head and go on his way, headed for Torrey Pines, I'm sure. I picked up on my friend from the Bimmer store standing in the back of the crowd.

"Hey Tanner! How ya fixed for used cars? The lady needs a ride."

"Just come on over and take whatever she wants and we'll take care of the paper work tomorrow."

When the cops finally cleared us to go, we walked over to the lot and a black, 2012 M6 X sports coupe caught her eye. The price tag said $46,999.

"I'll take it," Lucy said and Tanner went in to get the key.

"Isn't that a little over your budget?"

"My budget just got a whole lot bigger, thanks to your masterful driving. In fact, we should check real close. The insurance company that's covering that black SUV might just be buying me a brand new one. You know a good lawyer?"

"What do you think?" And I smiled my best smile.

We headed south down PCH and she wanted me to drive, for some strange reason.

"Do you have any idea what one of these sell for new?" I asked.

“In the neighborhood of 85 to 90,” she said.

“Wow!” I whistled. “That’s a pretty nice neighborhood.”

“I’m pretty sure whoever owns that SUV, a rental company or whatever will be tickled to death to get out of this for ninety thousand plus med bills. I'd say you're in line for a pretty good payday as well old timer.”

“I’m sure your right,” and I smiled again. So here it comes, Old timer. I should have known.

It was almost four by the time we hit north San Diego, and I pulled into the parking area of my cond.

“Well, lover! You sure do know how to show an old guy a great time,” I said with a smile.

“Are you dumping me?” she asked.

“Haven’t you had enough of me yet? I’ve wrecked your new car, got you shot at and I’m sure you're gonna be black and blue all over by morning.”

“Well, then, I’m going to need someone to rub the oil all around. And besides, I could use a Crown and a couple of slices of pizza along with a great view of the ocean, if you are interested in my company.”

“Well, I honestly don’t know what the attraction is, but by all means, come on in. What kind of pie do you like?”

“Oh, I could go for a Godfather's meat and veggie deluxe with some pepperoncini peppers and get a sixer of Guinness black beer.

“Sounds great to me.”

“I’m starting to stiffen up. I’m gonna get in the Jacuzzi. Tell them not to hurry, an hour or so. Then come join me, please.”

“Sounds like heaven. I’ll be right there.”

By the time I ordered, made cocktails, Crown, no ice, undressed and made it to the bath room, Lucy was just starting to step into the full, steaming bubbles and I had a good view of her back side, There were bruises beginning to show, from her calves to the top of her shoulders and that was just the back.

Oh, poor baby! I said, as she settled in with a moan.

I handed her a large hi-ball glass, the only thing that could come close to the healing properties would be good pot, and she took a very long pull on it. I settled into the other end of the very hot tub and drained about half of my glass. I closed my eyes and my feet slipped up between her legs and she moaned once again.

"Don't! Stop!"

"Sorry," I said.

"No! I mean, don't stop!" she said, as she closed her eyes again.

We both must have dozed off because the doorbell startled me and Lucy moaned as she tried to wake.

"Did anyone get the number of the steam roller that hit us?" I finally made it out of the tub and yelled, "Hold on! I'm coming!"

I managed to get Lucy awake and out of the tub. I dressed her in one of my old shirts, my wardrobe of choice for her lately, and I got her settled into a chair on the patio. Great pizza, ice cold black beer and a beautiful sunset...If only I didn't hurt so much.

"How about a kayak ride up the coast?" I asked.

"What's today?" she asked.

"Sunday," I said.

"No, No! What month?"

I laughed and said, "September."

"Maybe around January," she groaned, "or March."

Two more stiff Crowns and the next thing we knew, it was 9AM. My cell phone rang and startled me awake. It was Tanner wanting to sell another Bimmer.

"I don't think were in any condition to travel today. You'll need to put on your dealing hat and come over to my place."

I gave him the address and told him not to be in hurry. Lucy was starting to come around.

"How about a slice of cold pizza for breakfast," I asked.

"It doesn't sound all that bad. Any Guinness left?"

"I don't know, but I'll see."

Tanner showed up about 11:15 and he just stared at Lucy.

"Lucy, how can you look so marvelous after all that you have been through, and he looks like...."

"Hey, you do know I'm sixty, right?" I said.

"I would have bet closer to 85," Tanner smiled.

Lucy explained that she wanted to rent the black Bimmer until she got the insurance settled and she would purchase a brand spanking new one. Tanner was so happy he didn't even charge her to rent the used one.

"The check for the policy you have should be ready by the end of the week," he said. "I can get it over to you or hang on to it till you get a hold of the other insurance company."

"Just give me a receipt for it and hang on to it. Can you be a doll and help me with that insurance company thingy?" she asked.

Tanner was so interested in Lucy sitting around in my almost see thru shirt that she probably could have gotten anything she desired.

"As a matter of fact, I can. That SUV was rented from a leasing company that we deal with. Shouldn't be a problem."

Tanner left without taking his eyes off of Lucy until the door was completely shut. I smiled and shook my head.

"What?" Lucy asked with a big smile.

"Can you help me with that insurance company thingy?" I repeated.

"Well, I sure didn't want to deal with it. Did you?"

"No, but did you have to be so obvious in your manipulation of the poor guy?"

"You and I both know he wasn't paying attention to a word I was saying."

"Wait...do you do that to me?"

"Of course not, Roc. I would never try to manipulate you. Now, can you be a doll and get me another one of those Guinness beer thingies?"

She stood there with a pouty smile while she fidgeted with the top button on her shirt...uhh, my shirt. I smiled and thought the hits just keep on coming. I walked to the kitchen singing a song in my head from the Playmates. *'What is love, five feet of heaven in a ponytail...the cutest ponytail that sways with a wiggle when she walks.' 1958. '59* maybe.

BIRDIES & SAN DIEGO HEAT

The Back Nine

Hole 10
Grip It and Rip It

By three o'clock, we decided that a kayak ride up the coast might just be what we needed to loosen up some aches and pains. I broke out the twelve foot tandem ocean going rig from the store room and we did our best impressions of spastic people climbing stairs as we tried to settle into the kayak and push off. We were just about to throw in the towel when things began to loosen up. We made it about a mile up the coast and then turned for home.

"How you doing Doll face," I asked as I talked to the back of her head.

"Doing well, you ready to take it home?"

"Absolutely, you set the pace."

We reached full speed and were just about a quarter mile from shore when something hit the water just short of the kayak to my left. Then another splash hit on our right and another on our left, but much closer.

"What the hell is that?" Lucy asked.

"Just keep paddling while I try to get a fix on where it's coming from. We need to get to shore."

We were about twenty feet from shore when a round hit the back deck of the kayak just behind me. The sun was in my eyes and even with my shades on, it was too bright to make out anything. We hit the shore and sprinted all the way back to the beach in front of my condo.

"I'm really getting tired of this. Time to change the game. Are you ready to go home now?" I asked.

"Why, are you ready to get rid of me?"

We sat on the patio looking out to make sure we didn't see anything unusual. I called Chief Dan on my cell with the speaker on and I had a large Crown already working.

"Hey, Roc. What's up?"

"Damn it, Dan! Now they're shooting at me while I'm exercising! I've had enough! I'm coming out hard and strong and I need you to step up or step back so none of your guys get hurt."

"Hey, hey, hey...just calm down, Rocco. Do me a favor, stay low till morning and let me do my job. I'm sending over six uniforms, in fact, they are already on their way. They'll be outside your house all night and every one of my detectives are on this. I've got a call into the FEDs as we speak. I'm sure the FBI will be checking in with you very soon."

"Sorry Dan, didn't mean to loose my temper. It's just that it's been a couple of really bad days."

Lucy gave me a really hard stare.

"Uhh...with a couple of exceptions," I said with a little extra inflection in my words. It seemed to work.

“Not to worry, Roc. Have a couple of large Crowns and try to relax. I got this.”...and the phone went dead.

“Now to you,” I said as I looked Lucy in the eye. “What the hell is wrong with you? Are you just nuts or what?” I must have caught her off guard because she was speechless for a couple of long seconds. I watched as the shock wore off and her look went from a tired smile to total blank stare to anger, and finally to just flat out pissed off. I could tell she was about to let me have it so I continued.

“You're 19...or 20 and you're spending your time with a 80 year old man. I don’t know if you’re trying to make me stroke out or just drop dead of a heart attack and, and, and don’t you have any friends your own age...and what the hell is going on with you?”

Lucy slowly stood and faced me. The setting sun was coming through different areas of the very thin white dress shirt that she had on, and all of a sudden, my anger started to fade. Unfortunately, I couldn’t say the same for hers.

“First, I’m not nineteen, I’m thirty one, and you’re only sixty. And second, you son of a bitch, if you don’t want me in your life, I’m gone!”

The few buttons of my white shirt that were actually buttoned, flew in all directions as she ripped it open and tore it off throwing it to the floor of my small patio. I knew immediately that I would regret this and hoped maybe someday she’ll forgive me. Watching her walk away hurt even more, her bruises showing brightly in the late afternoon sun. Was I upset that I was losing this gorgeous woman, or upset that her bruises were because of me? I should get up and follow her, I even tried once but the pain of all my injuries from the crash put me back down in my chair. About thirty seconds later my front door slammed and the entire condo rattled. I forced myself to get up and check to see if the front door was still on its hinges. I got to the front door and opened it, about to yell for Lucy, and a thirty something man in a very nice business suit was standing there trying to look around me into the room.

"Excuse me Sir, is Mr. Reese here?

"I'm Mr. Reese," I answered, and he was taken aback for a moment.

"I'm sorry Sir; your granddaughter said you were on the patio."

"That wasn't my granddaughter, it was my barber," I said with enough sarcasm that he knew he had screwed up.

"I'm sorry Sir. Can we start over? I'm Bill Kelly with the FBI, may I come in?"

"If you stop calling me 'Sir'."

I poured myself another stiff Crown and offered my new young friend something. He declined.

"Great view," he said as he looked out over the Pacific. "When I get old, I'd like to live in a place just like this."

Then he turned red, and looked over at me. I was frozen, head cocked to one side with my drink in my hand just staring at him.

"I'm sorry, Mr. Reese. I didn't mean...."

"Stop!" I put my hand up. "Don't worry bout it. If you do you'll be pulling your foot out of your mouth the rest of the night. And we can't keep starting over."

"Right...okay...?"

"Why don't you just ask me what you came here to find out?"

"Yeah, uhh...can you give me your view of what's going on, Mr. Reese?"

"What's going on is someone is shooting at me and my barber and I'm getting really pissed off and need it to stop. It's about to give me a heart attack. And call me Roc."

"Excuse me, Roc. But you don't look like the type that gets rattled or scared to easily."

I told him of Neil and the shooting at Ray's that I thought probably came from his office. I told him of the shooting at the restaurant on the beach, the car crash in La Jolla and then the shots on the kayak. Young Mr. Kelly was video recording everything I said on his cell. All I could think about was that Lucy was out of the picture and safe, for the moment!

"And don't forget to keep and eye on my barber," I said.

"It would be my pleasure," he replied as he was leaving.

I laid around for a couple of hours, half trying to sleep but half wanting to call Lucy. I knew I couldn't but life was sure moving slower without her. About 10:30, I covered my entire body in Blue Emu ointment, took one last pull to finish off my Crown and hit the nest. I don't know if it was the Crown, the paddle up the coast or the Blue Emu, or maybe the FEDs and cops outside, but I slept the sleep of children; although, I did kind of miss having my barber in my arms, like a big ol' teddy bear.

I opened my eyes about 6:30 and just laid there, kind of afraid to move cause I knew how much it was going to hurt. I tried to wiggle one toe and then tried to move to the edge of the bed. I dropped my right leg over the side, and...,

"ohhuhhoww, CRAP!"

I know for a fact that at a certain point your nerves will go numb and you can't feel anything. That didn't happen to me. I feel everything. I remember dreaming about a group of guys all pounding on me with baseball bats. Not quite sure it was a dream. I managed to stand to my feet but I couldn't put my pants on and I was so happy that the only socks I own are in my golf bag. I wiggled like a penguin over to the patio door, flopped into a chair and reached for my coffee cup.

"Crap!"

I didn't have a coffee cup. I thought for a couple of seconds then I picked up my cell phone and pushed # 4.

"Club house, this is Nancy."

"Oh Lord, Nancy...its Roc, I need your help."

"Sure Roc, anything...what can I do?"

"Can you bring me a couple of those large Styrofoam water cups full of coffee, the way I like it?"

"Sure sweetie, anything else?"

"Yeah, bring a pass key 'cause I don't think I can answer the door, I'm on the Lanai."

"You got it, Doll face. Give me a couple of minutes and I'll be there. By the way, saw you on TV yesterday and the day before!"

"How'd I look?"

"Sweetie, you always look good. On my way up."

At this minute I would sleep with Nancy over Lucy. I love this woman, this eighty-something, gorgeous, bringer of life to my door. I LOVE YOU, NANCY! My phone rang just as I was trying to set it down. It was Tanner from the Bimmer dealership.

"Hey Buddy! What's up?"

"Hey Roc, Lucy's here and she wanted me to give you a message."

"Great, what is it?" I asked.

"She wanted me to let you know that I am her friend now, and that anything you need from me will need to go through her first."

"What? What are you talking about?"

"I know it doesn't necessarily upset the delicate balance in your world, but Lucy wanted to make sure I said this to you in front of her. I told her you wouldn't care."

"So you do everything she says now, Tanner?"

"How much money have you spent with me in the last 3 days?"

"Well, Nothing I guess."

"Yeah, well Lucy has spent a lot. I mean a lot. And if she wants me to be her friend instead of yours, then I'm her friend. Besides, she is much prettier than you."

Just then Nancy set two giant foam cups on my patio table and kissed my forehead and waved as she left.

"Ask Lucy if she's finished sending me messages? I have some very large coffee cups with my name on them."

"Yeah, she's through, but she really is pissed," Tanner said.

"Good!" Just as I was about to hang up, I heard him talking.

"Hey Roc, we still on for golf next Thursday?"

"Of course, we just aren't friends anymore. Take care, man."

"You too, friend...I mean not-friend...whatever."

And I hung up and tried to reach for a cup of Life, it was all I could do to lift it. It felt like a twenty five pound dumbbell, and I felt like a 185 pound dumb bell. Go figure.

By the time I had finished half of the second giant cup of Joe, I was beginning to feel about halfway normal, albeit the bottom half. At least it was about four hundred per cent better than when I climbed out of bed a few hours ago. I sat in the hot hot shower for about ten minutes and then did a full body rub down with Blue Emu. I was finally able to get into my pants and shoes and head out the door. Don Williams came to mind and I tried to sing as I walked, "Lord, ouch...I hope this...ouch...day is good...ouch."

I don't think I have ever felt this bad. I have aches and pains on my aches and pains. Every time I moved I wanted to scream and I hadn't even made it to my car yet. Coming around the corner I could see it up ahead, but something didn't look right. And then I saw it, four flat tires. Normally I would be fuming right now, but normally this would be punk kids or possibly a former girlfriend. Wait, was this Lucy? I stood there and thought for just a second. No. No way. She is way too classy for this. This was someone trying to send a message. A message like, 'hey, get some new tires.' Well, okay. I needed new tires anyway. I was hurting and ticked off but I was trying to look on the bright side, the side that says, "I am going to kick this guy's ass when I find him.' I wasn't quite sure how much they knew about me, but now I know. I grabbed my phone.

"La Jolla BMW," the voice on the phone answered.

This is Rockland Reese, let me talk to the owner.

"Yes, sir, Mr. Reese, one minute please."

"Roc! Not sure I have permission to speak with you, but Lucy is still here, I'll ask her."

"Shut the hell up and put me on speaker. Someone slashed all four of my tires. Was it her?"

I could hear Lucy in the background, "Of course not. I would never do that to him."

"She say's no," Tanner said.

"I didn't think so. Well, I need a truck with four new tires out here A-S-A-P."

"On their way, Roc."

I hung up.

"Good morning Mr. Reese."

I turned, and my new friend from the FEDs was standing there. I guess he was feeling pretty good about the fact that his guys protected me all night and I wasn't dead.

"Kelly...you're the one in charge of this whole thing, Right?"

"Yes Sir, I guess I am. What can I help you with?"

I just pointed at my tires.

"Do those look normal to you?"

"Oh my!" he said.

"Oh, my? Is that the best you've got? Who was watching the front of my place last night? I want to meet the genius, where the hell is he?"

"Well, he works nights, so I'm afraid he's off for the day."

"Kelly! Come with me."

I led him to the club house

"Nancy Sweetheart, would you please open the electronics room for me?"

"Of course Roc, anything for you, my love," and she pulled a large key ring from the front pocket of her apron. She opened the door wide and backed out motioning for us to go in.

"Just let me know when you're done, Roc," Nancy said as she headed back to her desk.

"Thanks Nancy. Shouldn't be long."

We sat looking at the monitor that was displaying the parking area. I scrolled through in fast forward until I saw something at 2:17 am. I went back slowly and saw a dark figure in a hooded sweatshirt with a bandana over his face kneeling by my right front tire.

"Kelly boy, does that look like the body of a female to you?"

"No Roc, it doesn't and look at the size of those sneakers. They're at least elevens."

We watched the dark figure poke holes in all my tires and then move to the left out of the frame of the camera. I noticed two cars away from the exact spot my slasher exited sat a big, black Ford Excursion.

Pointing to the monitor I asked, "Does that idiot there belong to you?"

"Not for long," Kelly replied, and he pulled his phone and started pushing buttons very rapidly.

"Get your ass back here, now!" and he hung up.

Wow, I didn't think he had it in him.

"Well, as fun as this has been, I've got things to do. I'll leave you to it," I said and got up from my chair to leave.

"I'll take care of it Mr. Reese...uh Sir...umm Roc."

I left him in the video room and walked outside to wait for my tires. Just then, a brand new silver M6-X BMW came sliding around the corner and into the parking lot. It stopped just at the rear of my slightly lower than normal LS460. The passenger window came down about half way and I heard a very familiar voice.

"Hey Sailor, how about some breakfast?"

"You do know I'm doing my very best to keep you from getting shot, don't you?"

"I have to admit, it took me a while, but I finally figured it out. I'm sorry about yesterday. Get in."Lucy replied.

"I'm not sure that is such a good idea. This is getting pretty serious, and you need to stay away from me."

"Shouldn't that be my decision?"

"I don't know," I shrugged.

"...or you could wait here for your tires. I'm sure they'll have you fixed up in a couple of hours."

Hole 11
Beach

I got in and sat on dark saddle colored luxury leather seats. Her perfume was floating very lightly in the air and she looked like a trillion dollars. Amazing...just amazing. I can't think of another way to describe her.

"Nice ride. About a 100k?" I asked.

"Not even close. I had thirteen hundred left over, or I mean the insurance company did. Your friend had everything ready when I got there."

"You mean your friend that used to be my friend?"

"She kind of blushed, "Yeah, sorry about that too."

We ate at a little place just across the Coronado Bridge that I didn't even know existed. The food was really good; Eggs Benedict made with crab instead of Canadian bacon on fresh made Sourdough rolls instead of English muffins and cranberry juice, and of course, more hot joe.

"Don't you work any more?" I asked.

"Well, I'm kind of in transition at the moment."

"What exactly does that mean?"

"Well, I heard from your friend at the Interior Design Society this morning, and she offered me a job at three times what I make at Jaxon's, and I do pretty well."

"Well, that's great because you're kind of getting too

old and wrinkly to be a waitress."

I got a kick in my shins. Fortunately, I hurt in so many other places that I hardly noticed.

"You may have to buy some new clothes, the days of but cut shorts might just be over."

"Yeah, about that...Roc, I've been thinking about going into business for myself."

"I hear a huge favor coming."

"Roc, you know everyone on the coast and I could use a partner to get me started," she said thoughtfully.

"What kind of business?"

"I was thinking, maybe in sales. People want to buy things and we could find the things they want to buy and sell to them. What do you think?"

"That's pretty sketchy," I said. "You do know I'm a golfer by trade, don't you?"

"Sure, but you can only play golf once or twice a week. You could work for me the rest of the time."

"Work for you? I thought you just said a few seconds ago that you wanted me to be your partner?"

"Oh yeah, well that's just semantics."

"Not to me. Which is it? Work for you or be your partner?"

"Ah, Work for me of course."

"Not interested."

"Okay, fine...partner with me."

"Well, that's different...Not interested."

"Come on Roc. Why not?"

"Listen Sweetie, when I'm not being shot at and helping young girls buy cars, I play golf seven days a week."

"Seven days a week? Don't you get tired of not doing anything? Don't you want to make money? Don't you want to have a job?"

"I have a job, I'm a golfer. That's all I have ever done since I was 13."

"A cook at Jaxon's plays video games in his free time. It's all he talks about. But even he knows that he has to make some money to survive. Time to grow up, Dear."

"You don't understand, I play golf for money."

"What... little five and ten dollar bets? How much can a seventy year old man make playing golf?"

"I'm sixty, and last year I claimed two hundred and sixty thousand on my tax form, and probably hid another hundred and twenty in cash that I lived on."

"What? Three hundred and eighty thousand dollars playing golf? I thought it was just a game," she said.

"Oh, it is a game my dear. It's the number one sport there is, and if I were still in my forties I could play all over the world for a whole lot more."

"Shut up. Are you serious?"

"As a heart attack," I said. "Jordan Spieth has won around twenty-six million so far this year and that just golf, not all of his endorsements."

"Who?"

"Never mind, let's get back to this fairy tale of yours."

"No, no, no...Jordan who?"

"He's a twenty two year old golfer, number one in the world. My grandson played him five times in Dallas junior golf and beat him three times.

"Is that good?"

"Come on sweetie, concentrate, number one in the world and my kid kicked his ass three times."

"Is he going to play golf for a living?" she asked."

"We're working on it. He's at TCU now but he plays a lot at Colonial with Ryan Palmer. Apparently they met at church and Ryan kind of took him under his wing. Yeah, he'll play golf."

"Who's Ryan Palmer?"

"Just one of the best...never mind."

"I have gone to the driving range a couple of times with some friends just for fun and they said I was a natural. I didn't really take it too serious. But I've actually never been on a golf course. Do you think I could go with you some time?" she asked.

I had to think about it for a second. Jeanie used to always want to go with me. I loved her more than life itself, but golf was different. It wasn't really a place for us to be 'us'. I never asked to go to her book club. I just thought that we had our own things. I would flirt with the cart girls, tell bad jokes and drink way more than I should, and I just didn't want Jeanie's condescending look all day. I realize now how much time I lost with her. I always new we would grow old together, but I wasn't doing the 'together' part very well. I realize now how much time I lost with her. There was also another side to this...there isn't a senior in southern California that could draw a club back while Miss Lucy was standing around in short shorts.

"Any time you want Doll face, any time you want."

"So what do ya think partner? Can we make some money together?"

I thought of the possibilities and wanted to ask if she had any friends that looked even close to as good as she did. Then I thought better of it, and let the images of being the number one pimp on the Southern California coast just fade away. I do believe I would give up golf for that.

"I'm sure we can find something to do to make a buck," I said. "In the meantime, you need to go into the Interior Design Society and learn everything you can about the business. There's a lot of money in Southern California that gets spent on furniture and accessories and after she gets you trained, you tell her you want to be an independent. They'll be pissed but they'll go for it."

"What are you going to be doing?"

"Playing golf, Sweetheart. You need to take me back home. I have some Mexican Banditos that can't wait to meet with me."

"You need to be very careful, Roc. You're not as young as you used to be."

"Yeah, but they don't know that."

She laughed just a little and said, "This isn't funny. Maybe I should stay here tonight."

"Can you cook, girl?"

"What do you think?"

"Well, maybe we could do a trial thing for a spell," and I walked off.

The BMW guys were just finishing up on my car when I came back down from brushing my teeth. I went ahead and got another magazine for my Glock and thought about bringing my 19 as well that would give me another 15 rounds at hand, but I brushed it off and went on my way. $1200 for Michelin tires and I was steaming again, but at least I was on my way. I called Neil and we met for coffee.

"You need to stay close to the ground, Son. These guys, whoever they are, are not afraid of anything. They tried to take me out on one of the busiest highways in the country with no hesitation."

Neil was way too big to be the midnight tire stabber and was a truly nice guy, or so I was beginning to believe. It took an hour to go over what was beginning to come together in my head, Neil had a couple of questions that got me thinking, but all in all he was convinced I was on the right track.

"Oh yeah, hey Roc, did I tell you how good you look in high def?"

I just gave him the one finger salute over my left shoulder and kept on walking as I reached for my cell phone.

"Hey Roc, what's up?"

"Hey Dan, just making sure you're there. I'm headed your way to check out those tamales."

"I'm here, come on."

Fifteen minutes later we were in the morgue looking at two naked Mexican bandits.

"Their fingerprints have been sanded off and the only thing that we had to go on were their tattoos, and they were home made at that. They both had one that was pretty close to being the same; an eagle with a skull in its mouth flying over crossed pistols and some Mexican gibberish underneath," Dan said.

"Figure out what it means yet?"

"Of course...we traced the tats to a very large gang out of Santa Rosalia, Mexico. Looks like they're into exporting pot, cocaine and just about any other illegal substance that the American people are hooked on."

"Looks like poor old Ray was involved in some things that were above his pay grade. Maybe he was trying to take over or maybe get out, either way not a good decision."

"A recipe for disaster, I'd say," said Dan.

Maybe it's my age, maybe it's the aching from the car wreck, or maybe it's just that time of day...but I needed a drink. I headed towards my condo, knowing with police protection, I could relax and let my guard down just a bit.

Sitting on the patio with a Crown in my hand, I almost fell asleep with my eyes open watching the sunset. As beautiful as it was, I couldn't stop thinking about the case. I could hear the waves softly crashing to shore in between Lucy's steady breathing in the chair next to me.

"Have you ever spent any time in Mexico?" I asked.

"As a matter a fact, I lived in Puerto Vallarta for three years when I was a teen ager."

"Ever been to Santa Rosalia?" I asked.

"Yep, several times. It's a sleepy little town full of nothing but drug pushers and prostitutes. I used to work there."

"Excuse me?" I questioned.

"Just seeing if you were paying attention."

"So you speak Spanish?"

"Yeah, and I'm pretty good at it too."

"I'm sure you are," I said. "Looks like I'm going to need an interpreter. You interested?"

"When are we leaving?" She asked.

"First thing in the morning. I wonder if they have a golf course, 'cause we're gonna need a cover."

"Let me check and see."

She went to my computer and was back in less time than it would take me to turn it on.

"They have a championship course designed by Greg Norman, who ever that is? It's at the Baja Marriott."

"Can you make us reservations for tomorrow night?"

"I already did," she said.

"Well...how did you know I would want to stay there?"

"Because, it's a golf course." she said with a smart tone in her voice. "Besides, that's where I'm staying."

We heard a timer go off in the kitchen and as I turned to look Lucy said, "Dinner is ready." We dined on grilled snapper in butter sauce, broccoli and tomato salad with a vinaigrette that she had made with honey and Grey Poupon mustard, and some Kings Hawaiian bread with baked garlic. Of course she can cook.

"I'm going home for a bit and grab some clothes and a passport and I'll be back by the time you get the dishes done."

"Ah, Crap!" So I've been relegated to doing the dishes before I can go save the free world? I should have known it was coming.

The next morning, just after sunup we had a couple of overnight bags and my clubs in Lucy's M6-X, and we were headed south on the 5 to the Mexican border.

"I hope you didn't bring your gun with you, we could end up in prison for the rest of our lives?" she stated.

"Don't be silly, I know that, that's why I hid them at the bottom of my golf bag." I almost went through the windshield when she slammed on the brakes.

"Roc! Are you crazy? You can't take guns into Mexico."

"I know, but you can't go to war with a tire iron either. Besides, they never check the bottom of my golf bag."

I tried to change the subject, "We probably should have taken my car. Some of the roads south of the border are pretty nasty."

"Not to worry," she said. "I got another one of those amazing insurance policies to go with this car too." We both smiled.

We made it through the border checkpoint with little or no problem. The border guard was so focused on Lucy he forgot to asked for our passports, and didn't care if I had any guns with me or not. We headed south about thirty miles and came to a roadblock manned with guys carrying automatic rifles, dressed in cammo uniforms and helmets,.

"What's this all about?" I asked.

"The army's in with the drug dealers and they keep a pretty close eye on folks traveling into Mexico, so don't be a smart ass, okay?"

"Okay, but pull your skirt up a couple more inches just in case."

She smiled but did it anyway. One of the uniformed army guys came to Lucy's window and looked in, and then held his hand up for us to stop completely, which she did. He signaled for the other men in the area to come over and they gathered around, all staring into the car, pushing and pulling to get a better look.

"Tell them you're taking you grandfather to a clinic to treat his cancer."

She didn't look at me; she just sat quietly and waited for them to get through. After a couple of very long minutes, they began to wander away and the one at her window said, "Pasar." She nodded and drove slowly through the cement barricades and back onto the open highway.

"Hey grandpa! Are you ready to drive yet?"

"Very funny. Pull over the next chance you get and I'll take over."

There were no speed limit signs that I could see so I kicked the new sports model up close to 90 and moved on down the highway. *'Moving ahead so life won't pass me by.'* I love Jim Croce.

We pulled into the coastal area of Santa Rosalia about four in the afternoon and checked into the

Marriott. It was nice but different than anything you'd find in the states; their idea of luxury is just not quite the same. We dined on Nachos with shrimp and goat cheese melted on top and Ceviche, a raw seafood cocktail cooked by pouring lime juice over it and letting the citric acid do its job. We sipped white wine, and a couple of shots of locally made Tequila that was as smooth as Lucy's...never mind. Finally, we split a very large filet mignon with flaming Brandy over it and some grilled asparagus and life was very good.

"I guess we need to go to the golf course in the morning and let them see that I really can play."

"What do you mean?"

"I'm pretty sure they are aware that we're here and they're suspicious." I ordered a new bottle of Tequila, some lime and salt sent to our room and we sat on our patio and watched the luminescence on the ocean. The Mexican version of the northern lights, I guess. I've heard it's caused by dead fish and stuff floating in the water, but whatever, it was nice to look at.

"Since we're partners, I think we should take off that robe," I said.

Lucy stood and turned to me and opened her Marriott emblemed robe and let it fall.

"Wow! I guess we'll know when the partnership is over, when you quit doing this," I said.

"Or when you quit asking," she said.

"Good point," I replied, and she took a shot of Tequila and bent down and kissed me.

Hole 12
Up and Down

Morning came way too soon.

"I'm going down to the golf course. Come on down when you're finished getting ready and we'll have breakfast."

She entered the club dining room wearing white short shorts and a mango colored halter top with matching medium high heels just high enough to make her calves pop, and accented with just the right amount of gold jewelry.

"Every single time I think you can't possibly look any better, here you come again. Wow."

"Why thank you, Pops," she said.

"Pops...?"

"Yeah, aren't you dying of cancer," she asked. "So what are we supposed to do now?"

"Well, I'm pretty sure someone will be looking for us before too long."

I putted for a while and let Miss Lucy stroke a few. She really did roll the ball well. We went to the driving range and I hit some wedges then I handed her the pitching wedge and she lined one up, took a couple of practice swings, waggled and then smoothed one high and down the line about ninety six yards just short of the 100 yard flag.

"Can you do that again?" I asked.

"What?" she asked.

"Hit another shot just like the last one?"

"I guess so, did I do something wrong?"

"On the contrary, you did something very right. Hit another."

I dropped another range ball in front of her and she waggled a little. That alone was worth the ten dollars for a bucket of practice balls. Then she turned and came back through hitting down on the ball like a pro and again, the ball flew through the air on a perfect arc and came to rest about two feet from the first. I handed her an eight iron and she went through the same set up and hit the ball about 130 down the line.

"One more," I said, and she repeated the shot almost exactly.

"How many balls have you hit?"

"Four, I think."

"Not just now," I laughed. "I mean, in your life."

"I don't know, maybe twenty or twenty five."

"You're messing with me, right?"

"No! Why would I?" she asked.

"...because you can?"

I went threw the bag with her, all the way to the driver and nearly every shot was pure as pie, not long but very pure. Just one amazing shot after another. It dawned on me that she was in heels and halter top with skin tight short shorts. What could she do if she had her own clubs and was dressed appropriately?

"Hey you, mystery lady, follow me."

We went into the pro shop and dressed her for golf; except for the white short shorts. I kind of liked them just the way they were, and they could give us one hell of an advantage if it came down to it.

"What is up with this?" she asked.

"Just hang with me for a few hours."

We went to the first tee, and I talked her through the par four hole with a five.

"Just relax and pretend you're just hitting them out on the practice tee, got it?"

"Yeah, got it."

She was a great student and a real talent. I talked her through the rest of the front nine and we broke for lunch. She shot a real time forty one and I was impressed as hell.

"Can I talk now?" she asked.

"Before you do, let me say a couple of things."

She just looked at me with a strange twinkle in her eye.

"I believe we just found something we can make a dollar or two at, Partner," I continued. "Tell me how you feel about what you did out there?"

"I absolutely loved it. It was the best feeling I've ever had. When that little ball comes off the club and you can't even feel it, that's the best feeling ever."

She looked in my eyes, "...except when I'm in your arms, of course."

"Do you know that ninety percent of all golfer never break ninety? Ever...and you shot a forty one. You want to get something to eat and go back out?"

"No!" she said.

"I looked disappointed but I understood. It's not something everyone can deal with or care about.

"No, I want to go now." She grabbed my arm and pulled me to my feet. "Come on, Pops."

The course was almost empty, so I spent a lot of time explaining shots and what to expect if you hit it where you wanted. She shot a legit thirty eight on the back, from the lady's tees of course. I explained to her, that I started playing when I was thirteen. I played seven full rounds and hit about a million practice balls before I broke eighty, and everyone said I was a natural.

"Of course, I didn't have me for a teacher," I said and we both laughed.

"Are you ready for something to eat now?"

"Yeah, then can we hit some more balls?" she asked.

"Even my grandson wasn't this eager to learn. Sure if that's what you want?"

"I want you to show me some more shots."

We were eating and I saw a couple of guys eyeing us from the other end of the bar, not exactly golfer types, not even in Mexico. We went to the range and I saw them again sitting on the patio at the club house keeping an eye on us, or at least on the lovely Lucy. I had a hard time keeping my eyes off of her myself.

"Can we play again tomorrow? Please, can we?"

"Well, if were still alive in the morning, I guess so."

She looked at me with a strange look.

"See those two over on the patio? They've been keeping an eye on us since we got off the course and probably before."

She incorporated a look into a practice swing so it wasn't too obvious. I watched her hit the rest of the balls in the bucket and we called it a day. We left our clubs and shoes with the guys at the pro shop and they started cleaning and polishing as they watched Lucy walk away.

"Why don't you go get cleaned up in the room and I'll meet you back in the bar," I said, and headed to the locker room for a steam and massage.

I made it to the bar first and ordered two double Crowns on the rocks just as Lucy made her entrance. I watched her walking over towards me and realized that she wasn't just beautiful, but she knew how to walk, dress and act like a lady. I was taken back to a conversation with my dad when I was a kid. We were sitting in his pick up just outside the bar on one of the main streets in town and he was looking at every woman that walked by.

"Rockland, do you know the difference in this woman and that one," he said as he pointed down the street.

"No Sir," I answered in a wobbly voice.

"This one is a lady, that one is a slut. A lady can pretend to be a slut, but a slut can never pretend to be a lady. Son, always be with a lady."

We were making small talk, actually golf talk when our friends from the patio walked up to the table.

"Mr. Reese?"

"Yes, I'm Rockland Reese. What can I do for you guys?"

"Our boss would like a word with you if you don't mind," he said with a slight Mexican accent.

I looked around and acted like I was looking for someone.

"Well, sure send him over."

"Uh...Mr. Reese, he's at the Hacienda, Sir. Mr. Juan Martinez would like you to join him for cocktails this evening at eight o'clock I'll be happy to pick you up at your hotel at 7:30, Sir."

I looked at Lucy and she shrugged back.

"Well my friend, I guess we'll see you at 7:30. I presume you know where to find us?"

He nodded and said, "Yes sir."

"Yeah, never a doubt," I mumbled to no one particular.

We got up to our room and I had Lucy Google Juan Martinez of the Santa Rosalia Martinez's and surprise, surprise! There he was; business man, entrepreneur, family man, and all around good Samaritan.

"Uh...what about drug kingpin, extortionist, slave trader, murderer...any thing like that?"

"Calm down, Papa. You'll bust something."

"So is that the new thing? PAPA?" I asked.

"Don't you like it?" she asked.

"Not so much. Why don't we try partner?"

"We'll see."

"Have you ever fired one of these?" and I tossed the Glock 26 on the bed.

“No, never,” she said.

“Oh Lord, I hope your quick study didn’t end on the course today.”

I put her through a very fast self defense and handgun course, and as usual, she took to it like a duck to water. We showered and cleaned up from the day and as I was walking out of the bathroom I noticed Lucy taking a little black clutch from her duffel and out of it she pulled what looked like a handkerchief. She gave it a shake and the next thing I knew she was slipping into a shiny little black dress that sparkled when the light hit it just right.

“If I hadn’t just seen that, I never would have believed it. What...are you a magician as well?”

She smiled and wiggled a little and everything settled into place. A pair of black heels and just the right amount of gold accessories and she looked amazing. At exactly 7:30 there was a sharp knock at the door. Our new friend from the bar was standing there all washed and shiny in a fresh suit and tie with a smile on his face.

“Mr. Reese, Miss Barnes, how are you folks this evening?”

We arrived at the hacienda at two minutes to eight and walked through a beautiful courtyard with a cactus garden and Bougainvillea trees in all shades, blooming everywhere. We crossed a small bridge over a really big fish pond with large Koi begging for their dinner. There were men in business suites at each corner of the court yard and I knew for a fact they were all packing heat. Our guide led us through to the main room where our host was waiting with his family.

Juan Martinez greeted us along with three young boys, from ages maybe six to around thirteen, all clean and dressed in navy blue slacks and starched white guayabera shirts. Then there was Martina Martinez; one beautiful lady, maybe 38 or 40 with long black hair that ran down to her waist. She was dressed to the nines in a very tight burgundy skirt and matching heels and a white flowing silk blouse with lots of gold and diamond jewelry. She was beautiful, but not quite as beautiful as Lucy, and you could see that she knew it. We all shook hands and a servant appeared from out of nowhere with a tray full of drinks. Lucy and I were handed very large cocktail glasses with top shelf Crown and large chunks of ice.

A young Mexican lady led the boys off and we started the customary tour. Of course, it was a beautiful home with incredible views of the area. All the rooms faced the ocean with sliding glass doors, and the breeze coming off the water was wonderful. Martina and Lucy became fast friends and they walked off to who knows where. Juan and I walked into his study and sat in over stuffed leather chairs with a new cocktail handed to me every time mine got below half full. No trouble tonight, not in his home with his family there. I'm sure he thought the same thing and that's probably why they didn't even check us for firearms when we arrived. I took a deep a breath and relaxed a little.

Juan and I talked about BMWs, fast boats, race horses, golf and liquor; just about everything that I cared about. How did he know? We sat down to dinner at exactly 10:30 in the large dining room that would have easily seated twenty. We all sat at one end of the massive hand carved table and two well dressed Mexican young ladies served shrimp cocktails with fresh limes and hot tostadas, and a very fine red wine from a decanter. Juan could see that we were impressed and enjoying ourselves.

"A very nice round of golf today Lucy, 79, very impressive," Juan said. "How long have you been playing?"

Not knowing if we needed keep up any appearances, Lucy looked at me with concern.

"Tell him," I said looking over at her with a soft smile to let her know that she can relax.

"Today was my first round."

"No, No! I don't mean since you got to Mexico. I mean, when did you learn to play the game?"

"Really, Roc just took me to course for the very first time today."

Juan just sat there with his mouth open and speechless. "This I have to see. We must play tomorrow. I have a private course down the coast a few miles and no one will bother us. Martina plays as well, and we'll have a wonderful day. My driver will pick you up in the morning at 11."

I smiled and shrugged, but Lucy was bubbling with excitement.

"I can't wait," she said.

We finished our dinner and closed out the evening with Juan continually talking about his amazement of Lucy's golf game and how he was really looking forward to it. He must have mentioned it to his head of security three different times. That's when I realized that we were never supposed to make it back to the hotel. He had planned our demise for the trip back. Well, we could sleep safe tonight.

The next morning we were up early and had coffee, fresh juice and some fruit on our patio. I was going over what we might expect.

"I don't see him trying anything while we are all together. I'm sure he keeps any killing stuff away from his wife, not that she doesn't know what he does. I imagine we'll need to be ready tonight or on our way home. Just stay alert and keep that shooter in your purse."

Lucy wore khaki short shorts, a skin tight golf shirt with white background and blue, orange and yellow stripes running horizontally and a gold necklace. *'You're so young and beautiful and I love you so.'* Oh yeah, sing it Elvis.

"What about our clubs?" Lucy asked.

"Don't worry. They're probably on carts at Juan's club already."

Hole 13
Blind Hole

The foyer of the hotel was busy with people at ten to eleven; some checking out, some checking in and some just hanging around after a late breakfast. We made our way to the front door and a long black Cadillac pulled up just as I was looking at my watch.

"Exactly eleven o'clock," I said out loud to nobody in particular.

The other guy from the bar yesterday got out and opened the rear door. We entered to find Juan and Martina with big smiles and expensively dressed, ready for golf.

The ride down the coast was full of small talk that would have been a nice chat if I liked this guy at all. When we arrived and exited the car, I saw Lucy's bag on the passenger side of Martina's cart and mine was on Juan's. I pulled Lucy close for a last minute word.

"Just relax, and ask if you have any questions. I'll be close by."

Juan watched every shot Lucy hit and just shook his head each time. Her only really bad shots were when I gave her the wrong club and the ball flew over the greens. We played in about four and a half hours and Lucy shot another 79. Martina shot 93 and that would have been a good score if Lucy hadn't been showing off. We had cocktails and hors d'oeuvres in the beautiful club house and then rode back to our hotel. The ladies hugged and Juan and I shook hands. I heard Martina tell Lucy that we must keep in touch. I smiled on the outside but I was laughing on the inside. We watched the big black limo pull away.

"Now is the time to really be aware. They'll be coming before we get out of town."

I ordered room service that evening and we both slept with one eye open.

The next morning we woke early from a terrible nights rest. We grabbed our bags and headed for the front desk to check out. The front desk clerk handed me my car keys as I approached him.

"Good morning, can I have my bill please?"

"What is the name, Sir?"

"How did you know to give me this set of car keys if you don't know my name?" I asked.

"Yes Sir, your name please?"

"Reese! Rockland Reese."

"I'm sorry Sir, I don't have any record of you being here."

"I was in room 103, just around the corner."

"No Sir, that room has been empty for four days Sir. We haven't rented that room because of repairs."

Lucy came up behind me, "What's going on, Roc?"

"We've never been here, no record of us staying. Now it begins" I said. "Watch your back, Sweetie."

The phone rang and the clerk turned and answered it. As he was turned away I noticed another set of the distinctive BMW keys on a ring with a label that said 'Sandoval-Silver-BMW128i'. The desk clerk turned to me and asked, "Mr. Reese, is it?"

"You know it is."

"You have a call. You can take it over there at the house phone." He pointed to a stand and a white phone with a red flashing light. I walked over, slowly scanning the room for anything that might be out of place, and picked it up.

"Mr. Reese?"

"Yes, this is Roc Reese. Who is this?" I asked.

"This is Juan Martinez. I normally do not do this, but I truly enjoyed our day yesterday, so I just wanted to let you know that I know why you are here and I want to give you a warning; be very careful on your way home." And the phone went dead.

"Who was that?" Lucy asked.

"That, was our host, saying we probably wouldn't make it out of town. Let's go."

We ran to the car and opened the trunk. As Lucy was climbing in on the passenger side, I called softly to stop her.

"Lucy, stay down low and come help me."

I began moving all our bags to the car right next to us. It was a silver BMW 128i about 5 years old. Not anything like what we came in, but hopefully it would get us home. "Thank you Mr. Sandoval."

"What are we doing?" Lucy whispered. "I want my car."

"No you don't," I said.

At this moment I wished I was driving a new super BMW sports model, but at least it was a Bimmer and I had confidence that it would get the job done. Maybe we wouldn't be seen at all. As we pulled out of the parking lot and onto the main highway heading north, we heard a loud explosion behind us. It shook the road we were on and I was glad to be in a 128i.

"What was that?" Lucy half yelled.

"That my dear is the sound of a BMW M6 X being blown up with nobody in it."

"How did you know?"

"The desk clerk was a little too eager to give me the keys. We might just be okay."

"I'm so glad we are partners," she said taking a deep breath and exhaling in relief.

We had just passed the city limits when all hell broke loose. One of the rear tires exploded and bullets riddled the trunk lid of Mr. Sandoval's BMW. Lucy looked at me and said, "You're the worst driver ever!"

"You better get ready to run," I replied.

I took the first road I came to and headed down towards the beach. The rear of the car was fishtailing as I tried not to apply too much brake and put us in the ditch. More bullets ripped across the hood, and the engine coughed and sputtered and then died. I pushed the gear shift into Neutral, hoping the car would coast on down the hill as far as the water. The worn out piece of German crap left us stranded about thirty yards short of the dock. I could see a bright red and white cigarette boat tied at the end of the pier and I hoped we could make it; a total of about fifty yards down to the end, no cover, in the open all the way. I looked behind me and Lucy was getting out of the car. I was low on energy and air as I pointed at the boat and told Lucy to run and she blew by me like I was running backwards. I reached the dock and half a dozen bullets hit the wood and tore holes in the planks by my feet as I ran. It made me laugh, as I thought of the old time movies where the bad guy would shoot at the floor in the saloon and make the town drunk dance. Somehow, I made it to the end of the pier and into the boat. I was about to tell Lucy to keep her head down but she had already found the keys, fired up the engine and was untying the moorings. I was trying to talk, laugh and breath all at once without much success. Just then, Lucy pushed the throttle forward and I shot backward into a tuck and roll leather seat and we were off at breakneck speed. She ignored the five mile per hour speed limit inside the harbor and we hit the breakwater at close to seventy. I finally regained my breath and pulled out my cell phone and tried to make a call; no signal.

Lucy looked at me and asked, "Is it on Out of Country Roaming?"

"Out of what, what?

She handed me her phone.

"What's the number for 911?" I asked.

I checked my phone and got Chief Dan's number and dialed it. "Oh hell yes! Reception."

While it was ringing, I looked behind me and down into the hatch. It was stacked with large bundles of freezer bags.

"Oh crap!"

"What?" Lucy asked.

"I'm pretty sure we just stole one of Juan's shipments of drugs to America."

"This is Dan."

"Dan, this is Roc Need some help."

"Where are you, Rocco?"

"We just left the breakwater of Santa Rosalia, Mexico headed north at seventy miles an hour and Miss Barns is driving her ass off. You should see it, and when you get off the phone, will you call Tanner at the Bimmer store and tell him Lucy needs another new car, just like the last one?"

"What happened, Roc?"

"Long story, just suffice to say C4 can really make a mess of a brand new BMW.

"C4?" he asked.

"I don't know, maybe C5. Anyway, I have a feeling we're about to have a chopper coming up our butt any minute."

"What do you want me to do, Roc?"

"Hell, I don't know, call someone; the navy, the FEDs, the Coast Guard. I just don't want to be buried at sea."

Just then I heard a rotor coming up from behind.

"Gotta go, Dan. Tell them to look for the wreckage of a red and white cigarette boat and lots of packs of Cocaine floating all over...and tell them to hurry!"

Bullets ripped up the middle of the boat and white flour like powder floated up from the deck and we drove right through it. I reached down and grabbed two life jackets and was trying to help Lucy on with hers while she drove just as a flurry of bullets ripped across the center of the boat. Lucy and I both were perfectly still staring at a hole in the dashboard that had a tiny little smoldering ring around it, just inches from us.

"That was close," she said.

The chopper flew right on by and I had a couple of extra seconds to go over my plan with Lucy...plan? Hell, I didn't have a plan, maybe an idea and a lot of hope.

"Baby girl, when that thing turns and comes back it's gonna have its gun trained right down the middle of the boat. When you see him start to fire, veer to the right and count to two then turn hard left until it has gone by, then back to straight and I'll set you up for the next pass when it comes from the rear. If we can last till he runs out of ammo or maybe we get some help we might survive this mess."

The chopper came at us again.

"Lucy! This time veer left and then hard right."

"Got it," she said.

The chopper came screaming and looked like it was just inches of the water.

"Get ready Love. Here they come. 1...2...3...Now!" and we turned to the left and then right and the bird flew by once more. We took some shots across the stern but nothing that caused any serious damage.

"Great job, Girl! You probably should have been driving the car," I said with just a little bit of smile.

"Now straighten out and get ready for another charge."

"Okay, I'm going right this time," she stated.

The chopper came at us from the front one more time. Lucy began her right turn just a little and then immediately cut the wheel hard left and I almost lost my balance but grabbed the handle on the frame to steady myself.

"I thought you said you were going right?" I yelled.

"I was but I figured they would expect that so I changed my mind at the last second."

The chopper swung to our right, but we caught a few rounds right through the rear of the boat and into the engine compartment. The powerful motor belched and stalled as some 50 caliber rounds hit some vital spots. I looked down in the hold and noticed some of the white plastic bag were now floating.

"Ah crap! Not good."

We were slowing down. I could feel it and I was sure the guys in the chopper could see it.

"We're gonna have to go into the water," I yelled. "When you do, I want you to float face down and only take a breath when the chopper is on the opposite side of you. Do you understand?"

"Yes, Love. I got it. Hey, I just want you to know, it's been a hell of a ride. Short, but lots of fun."

"Hey girl, it's not over yet. Hell, I've been in much worse situations than this."

"Oh really...?"

"I once had to pitch onto the green from sixty feet away, three feet directly behind a sixteen foot tall tree and I was on a severe down slope. I had $15,000 on the line and only one shot left to win."

"What did you do?"

"I won. Just do what I say and we may make it out of this mess."

"I'm with you, but I want to hear the rest of that story one day."

The sea was starting to run higher with white caps about five maybe six feet high and the boat was beginning to plow. We were still doing around 38 or 40 miles per hour but that was about half of what we should be doing to stay above the waves. The sky was turning gray and the winds were turning straight into our bow. Just then the chopper appeared, hovering off our port side.

"Shall we jump?" Lucy asked.

"Not yet, it has to look perfect."

And it did look perfect. I saw the next wave just about three seconds away and I turned to the chopper and looked the pilot right in the eyes. I raised my right hand and extended my middle finger. He obviously saw it because he let a volley of bullets fly into the ocean just feet away from our boat in a trail that led up to our bow just as the huge wave hit the side of the boat pushing it up on it's starboard side and allowing Lucy and I a chance to get into the icy cold water without the pilot seeing us jump.

Just as we jumped, the boat cracked in half. The front of the boat doubled under and the rest of the boat climbed up on top and began to tumble. Lucy and I flew threw the air and landed hard in the running ocean, between two waves just as the engine of the boat ignited. Fire, metal and wood flew everywhere. The chopper was blown back on its tail but the pilot recovered into a turn in the opposite direction. Making a huge circle over the water, the bird returned to check on its victory and flew by us slowly, but never firing a shot.

“You okay?” I asked.

“Define okay.”

“Alive.”

“I guess I’m okay...That, was your plan?”

“Sorry, I cut it a little close, but I guarantee they think we are dead.”

We were safe for the moment. We floated each time the chopper came in view and then we slowly paddled toward the visible part of the hull trying to reach some cover. We ducked under the water and came up under the up side down cigarette boats front section.

“I wish I had a cell phone that was dry right now,” I said.

“You can use mine. It has a Dog and Bone waterproof case on it.”

“Are you serious?”

“Yeah, I got it for kayaking.”

She reached in the pocket under her life jacket and pulled out her cell. I looked at recent calls and pushed Dan’s number and it actually rang.

“Rocco? Are you OK? Where the hell are you?”

“I’m actually under water Dan and I don’t know how long this phone is gonna last. We’re under what’s left of our boat and a chopper with a 50 caliber gun is circling us. How far out is our ride?”

“The US Customs and the FBI should be about five minutes out.”

“Okay, I hope they're coming in with guns blazing ‘cause I don’t want to have to come back down here to kick these guys ass.”

Five minutes is an incredibly long time when you're waiting under half a drug boat in icy water off the coast of a foreign country.

There aren't any sharks out here, are there?" Lucy asked.

"Lucy Barnes, you look amazing even soaked in salt water."

"You didn't answer my question."

"Listen! It's a big bird."

I ducked under the hull and came back up on the outside in time to see very large Huey chopper, white with orange stripes, a black nose and a blue logo, US Coast Guard. I saw a figure standing on the rail with a hand held missile launcher. Flames shot out the back and a missile out the front that started tracking and caught the smaller bird in just a matter of seconds. BAAAAM! The small chopper exploded into a million pieces and fell into the ocean. They lowered a crewman into the water near us and he grabbed Lucy, taking her up into the chopper. I was next and in the chopper before I even had a chance to think about it. These guys are good. I think I'm going to renew my membership into the Coast Guard Foundation.

We were on a small private plane back to the San Diego Airport and I kept my life jacket as a souvenir.

"What's so important about that life jacket?" Lucy asked.

I peeled back some of the heavy canvas cover to expose a couple of bricks of Pot.

"Roc, what are you doing with that?"

"Just a little something for recreational use," I explained. "It was a gift from our host."

"You, my love, are crazy. You just had the Coast Guard of the United States fly you and your drugs into this country. Do you know what they will do to you if they find out?"

"Then I guess they better not find out."

"By the way," she said, "did you have a wager with Mr. Martinez?"

"Just a small one."

"How much?" she asked.

"Just five thousand."

"Yea! That's good news, our first business deal as partners."

"Yeah, except for the bad news."

"What's the bad news?"

"It's in my golf bag."

"Yeah...?"

"In the trunk of that car on the beach."

And we laughed out loud.

Hole 14
Split the Fairway

Tanner at the BMW lot wasn't near as excited to see Lucy as he was a few days earlier.

"Ms. Barnes, you have managed to buy three cars from me worth approximately two hundred and thirty thousand dollars but actually only spent twenty five thousand. I don't believe we can offer you another insurance policy with this new vehicle, Sorry."

"I completely understand. Here's my insurance carrier's information," she said.

She turned to me and began a new conversation as Tanner went about with his paperwork.

"We need to go get me some new clubs."

"What about your new job?" I asked.

"I took an absence of leave. I have been shot at, blown up, drowned and anything else I can come up with."

"You mean a leave of absence?" I asked.

"If you say so," she smiled.

"I need to call Neil and meet with him for a few minutes."

"Not a problem."

He came around the corner and met us at Jerry's. I ran over our trip and what I had found out. I explained to him what his daddy was involved in and the reason he was killed, and I assured him that Bob Carlson had no idea what was going on and he was squeaky clean. Neil was glad to hear that and we made small talk for a while then I told him we needed to leave and buy my new business partner some golf clubs.

"Hey," Neil said, "I know where you can get a dozen sets; brand new and it won't cost you a penny."

We drove up to Neil's daddy's mansion and loaded as many sets of clubs and bags as possible in the back of Lucy's new Bimmer.

"How about I have the rest sent down to your condo later on today?"

"Thanks Neil, that's really nice of you."

"No problem, Roc. Besides, I'm never going to use them. Let me know how this mess ends so we can settle up."

"I'll be in touch," I promised.

We dropped off four golf bags in my garage and kept two that I thought looked good. Senior flex and ladies are very close to the same, so we were fixed up for the moment and we headed for the driving range.

"What are you going to do about our Mexican friend," Lucy asked.

"Unfortunately, I don't believe I'll have to do much of anything. I have a feeling we'll be hearing from Santa Rosalia before too long."

"Really...? You don't think he'll just assume we are dead?"

"Not a chance, Sweetheart. A ton of drugs, a very expensive boat, a helicopter and a couple of confidants, and I bet he even owned that hotel that he blew up with your car. He lost some face. He'll be coming back for us."

We hit a large bucket of balls and then had some lunch and hit another one. She seemed to be getting stronger and I was wearing out. I sat down on a bench with a cold Coors Light and talked her through another large bucket: high fade, high draw, low fade, low draw, high straight, low straight and the reasons for each shot. She caught on very quickly.

"A couple more days of practice and a couple of rounds and you'll be ready to go to work."

"Really Roc, are you serious?"

"As a heart attack, Doll face. If you can keep it around 80 and keep looking great in those shorts, we have a combination that's pretty much unbeatable. I'm gonna have JJ set us up with a match or two just to test the waters."

"What do I need to do?" she asked.

"Just stay in shape, practice and show me your breasts any time I ask." I paused in thought for a second, "Yeah, Yeah, that's about it."

She dropped her club to the ground, walked over very seductively and stood right in front of me, grabbing my neck with one hand softly on each side and pulling my head up just a little bit. Then she kissed my forehead and rubbed her breasts in my face just enough to get me breathing again.

"That will have to hold you over."

"That will," I answered.

"Maybe we should sleep at my place until this Mexico thing is over," she said.

"You may be right. Old Juan is probably going to turn up the heat when he finds out we are still alive."

"How is he going to know?"

"Oh, I've already sent him a message."

"You did what?"

"Listen, I would rather get this over with now, than to have to watch my back for who knows how long. Besides, this way we can control at least a little of the situation."

We stopped to see my friend at the gun range and pick up a couple of new Glocks; a 19 for me and a 26 for Miss Lucy. My friend let me have them without the ten day cooling off period.

"Just don't shoot till your legal," he said.

"Maybe I should have just bought a bag of rocks," I said, and he smiled.

We picked up some ear protection and four boxes of practice ammo and headed back to the indoor shooting range. Lucy took to shooting like she was born to it and she loved it.

"Roc, were gonna have so much fun," she said as I went and purchased 200 more 9mm rounds.

We left the range and since I was going to her place, we drove by my condo to get a change of clothes. As we pulled into the parking lot something looked wrong; my garage door was ajar.

"Stay here while I check," I said.

I punched in the code with my left hand, holding my Glock in my right ready to fire and the door started to rise. About half way up I saw the rear of a Lexus

LS460i with gold trim. Then I looked back and mine was in the parking lot.

"What the hell?" I said out loud to nobody.

I walked in and took a closer look, and along the back wall was bag after bag of new golf clubs. There were ten more bags plus the four that we had dropped of earlier. Every high end brand out there was now sitting in my garage; TaylorMade, Callaway, Titleist and on the workbench was a couple of remotes for the car and a handwritten note from Neil.

'Roc, thanks so much for all your effort. I don't play so you should have these and I noticed your old wreck so enjoy the ride. We'll get together soon to settle up. Very sincerely, your friend Neil.'

A brand new $100,000 car, about $30,000 worth of golf stuff and he wants to settle up? Rich people, I guess I'll never understand them. Lucy came in and looked around.

"What's going on in here?"

"New golf clubs, new car, all top of the line. I guess Neil is very grateful," I said. "I guess it was about time to get a new ride."

"You might want to hang onto yours for a back up. You do tend to go through cars pretty rapidly," she said.

"You might be right," I replied.

I woke at 6:30 and looked outside; no ocean. It took me a couple of seconds to remember where I was, then I saw Miss Barnes glorious body sleeping on top of the satin sheets and it all came rushing back.

'Slide off of your satin sheets, slip into your long soft mink. You know how to find my door and I know what you're crying for.' Thank you, Johnny Paycheck.

I got up and put the coffee on and just sat back evaluating how I got here in my life. My phone rang. I realized that I was staring at the clock on the wall. It was 7:30. I looked down at my caller I.D. and saw that it was my young friend from the FBI, Billy Kelly.

"Roc, its Billy. You up?"

"Yeah, been up for a while. What's up, Kelly."

"Got some info on Martinez for you. Can you meet me at the coffee bar around the corner?"

"Keep someone watching the apartment. I don't want anything happening to my business partner."

"Business partner? I thought she was your barber?"

"Shut the hell up, and order me a large coffee with three creams," I said and hung up.

Slipped on my pants and shirt and put my paddle holster in the small of my back. My Glock 19 was actually very heavy with 15 rounds in it but I felt comfortable knowing it was there.

"What's up Kelly? Any thing going on over at my place?" I asked.

"Nah, just those guys that delivered your new car and all that golf stuff. What's that all about?" he asked.

"It's a long story. Maybe one of these days when this mess is over I'll tell you about it over a couple of cold beers."

"I'd like that," he said.

"I got word that a couple of Martinez's bandito's came across the bridge last night about 10:00. We picked them up right away and had a tail on them the whole time, that's why I didn't call you. They're at the Holiday Inn over by your place and I guess they're sleeping in today 'cause I haven't heard anything from any of my guys yet."

"Maybe your guys are sleeping in," I said with a smirk.

"You had to say it didn't you?"

I shrugged and gave him a little smile.

"So what's the plan?" I asked.

"If you and Miss Barnes will go through your regular routine maybe they will make a move against you and we'll grab them."

"I don't think they are going to do anything until Martinez gets here. Besides, he's the one I want."

"What makes you think he'll be coming into the states?" Kelly asked.

"Because I embarrassed the hell out of him in his own town and got away with it. Besides I beat him out of $5,000 on the golf course too, and that's too much for a man like him to handle.

"Five thousand, I guess you're buying breakfast."

"Well, it's not as glorious as it sounds. The cash went up in smoke along with Lucy's new Bimmer and our clubs and clothes. I had just bought her that golf rig a couple of days before."

We talked a while longer and finished strategizing. I left Billy with a cup of Joe and a sweet roll and walked back to Lucy's. She was still sleeping like a baby and I didn't wake her. I grabbed another cup of coffee and sat down to clean the packing oil off our Glocks. I took a sip from my cup and looked over at the coffee maker in the kitchen; no little red light. Lucy's coffee pot was automatic and had shut off. By the temperature of my cup, it must have been about an hour ago. I got up and made a fresh pot just as she woke at about 10:45. She came up behind me and wrapped her arms around my chest.

"Have I mentioned how happy I am with you?" she asked.

"It's just coffee," I said.

"Oh Roc, I love your sense of humor, too."

We spent the day at the driving range and then putted for an hour and a half and she never tired.

"Want to take the new Lexus for a spin? We can get something to eat up the coast. I know this place on the pier in Oceanside that makes the absolute best fish and chips ever."

"Do I need to change?" she asked.

"Can you change into Elvis?"

She just stared at me. I shrugged and said, "Anything else would be redundant."

I only thought I knew what a luxury car was. The Lexus LS460i has got to be the most incredible vehicle in the modern world for under $200,000. We ate on the pier and enjoyed the fresh sea air, looked in some of the shops and then headed north on the PCH and the afternoon was amazing. I didn't let Lucy know about the two Ford LTDs, one gray and one black that were keeping us in view. Billy Kelly's boys, I hoped.

We drove into LA, moved to I-10 east and headed toward I-5 then turned back south. Two hours later we exited the 5 at La Jolla and got back to the PCH. One of my favorite drives in the whole country so we leisurely drove back toward home. We went through the intersection that had us sitting on the fire hydrant and Lucy looked over at me and smiled.

“You can put your head in my lap if you're concerned,” I said jokingly.

“Uh, you know I’m a lady, right?” she rebuked.

“I know. Sometimes I just go too far. I’m sorry,” I said with a little redness in my face.

Just then a black late model pickup truck cut us off and I reached for my Glock. It got past us, changed lanes and was out of sight in a few seconds. I looked at Lucy and smiled. We stopped by my condo and got our golf clubs out of Lucy’s car then went to the driving range just as the lights came on. We each hit a large bucket and then putted for about thirty minutes.

“Hey Roc...?”

“Yeah, Babe?”

“...that shot you were telling me about when we were in Mexico. Was that real or were you just trying to distract me?”

“I lie about a lot of things to a lot of people, but I never lie about golf.”

“Then how did you do it?”

“I took my 64° wedge and I hit away from the green, uphill. The ball went up over my head and sailed behind me over the tree and landed four feet from the hole which it proceeded to roll into.”

“Are you joking with me?”

“Not at all, I’ll teach you that one. It’s a money maker, especially when you do it. Are you hungry?”

We headed to Jaxon’s for cocktails and and a bite to eat. The bartender hugged Lucy and told her she looked marvelous. Lucy had been on the road all day, hit golf shots for an hour and a half and looked like she just stepped out of the day spa. I looked and felt like I had been run over by a golf cart and dragged for a mile or so down the fairway. We had three very large Crowns and then shrimp cocktail and split a dozen oysters on the half shell. The evening in San Diego was fantastic with just about the best weather anywhere. I paid the tab for the FEDs that were sitting around the restaurant and we left. We watched some TV while we sampled a little of Mr. Martinez's pot and it appeared to be top shelf. Lucy got up and walked over to the bedroom and stopped at the door.

"Coming?" she asked without even turning around.

I was sitting there watching her walk and didn't even realize my mouth was open and I was staring.

"Of course I am."

Hole 15
Pin High

I awoke to the door bell and loud knocking on Lucy's front door. I checked the clock as I walked through the front room; 5:47. I rammed a round into the chamber of my 19 and held it behind me as I opened the door. Billy Kelly was standing there in tennis shorts, flip flops and a tee shirt that read *'Duke Charles Western Author'*

"What's up, Kelly? Come on in."

We sat at the counter in the kitchen and talked as we waited for the coffee to brew.

"He's here! In town and ready for business. He crossed the border about 45 minutes ago and headed to his warehouse, probably to load up on weapons."

"I wonder where he wants this to go down," I said.

"I don't think he cares, as long as he gets you."

"Okay then. I guess it's time to put an end to this crap for once and for all. And Billy, I want Martinez."

"Roc, you know I can't promise you anything like that. I can't even allow you to be involved, not officially anyway. If Martinez just happens to get in your sights or we take him down and you put a couple of extra caps in his ass at the same time, well, that's a different deal, you got me?"

"Yeah, Kelly, I got you."

The alluring Miss Lucy wandered out of the bedroom rubbing the sleep from her eyes, wearing a very thin light blue cotton tee shirt that broke mid thigh. Kelly choked and spit coffee all over his chest. Lucy smiled and said, "Morning Billy!"

"Good morning, Lucy."

She poured a cup of coffee and headed back to bed with her cute little hiney wiggling as she walked.

"Where do you want to confront this guy?" I asked.

"What?" Kelly said, still very distracted.

"Martinez...where?"

"Somewhere, where we can control the population and isolate the bad guys."

"How about the driving range? The batting cages should be empty and we can keep everyone out of the way this early in the morning. I'm sure they have someone watching it and he'll know when we get there."

"We...?" Kelly asked.

"Yeah, you don't think I'm going to let Lucy get in the middle of this, do you? And I need an automatic rifle to put down in my golf bag, and change your shirt."

"I'll hook you up, Roc."

About 7:30 Kelly and I headed for the driving range.

"Wow! What a nice ride, Roc. I don't believe I've ever been in a car this sweet. What kind of work did you say you do?"

"I don't believe it ever came up," I said. "But I play golf for a living."

"You mean you're a professional golfer?"

"Not in so many words," I replied. "I have never played on tour, but I have made my living playing for money since I was 13. That's why I live in San Diego, there are tons of guys that truly believe they can play golf and some of them can, kind of, and they have the bank accounts to back it up. Ray Benson was one of those types. He lost $35,000 to me in one round and his partner, Bob Carlson lost $70,000 in two days. There's always someone that's willing to take a shot, and every day someone becomes a senior and thinks they're still a young man."

"I think some people would call that, a hustler?" he said.

"I suppose, but everybody gets a fair bet in my game. It just that they usually buckle under the pressure, the yips, you know?"

"I've heard of them, just never played enough or for enough to have experienced them. I guess I play like I have the yips all the time."

"You may be better off staying away from the course. If you get hooked on golf, it'll eat at you till you crack or lose everything. In some ways, it can be worse than drugs. You'll go play a stupid game instead of going to work and end up loosing the money that you didn't even make that day. And 90 % of golfers think they're much better than they are. But I never play anyone that can't afford to lose."

We carried our bags out to the shack by the range and got a couple of large buckets and a couple of steaming cups of Joe and started to loosen up. Kelly was using Lucy's clubs. They were a little short for him and the shafts would be too whippy if he were an accomplished player. I watched him hit a couple of shots and he wasn't good; one off the toe, high and dead right, one off the blade, low and skidding down the grass about 50 yards, a whiff.

"Don't put any marks on Lucy's clubs or you'll have to deal with her wrath."

"Actually, I'd love to deal with her, wrath or other wise, I just wouldn't want to have to explain it to my wife," Kelly said.

Just then a bullet ripped through the shirt sleeve and a little flesh of my right arm and hit Kelly hard in his right shoulder as he was bending to tee up a ball. He went down and I jumped down beside him. I tried to get a view of the shooter as I pulled him over to and under the cement bench, maybe from the roof above the men's grill but not sure. I heard more gunshots, probably the bad guys 'cause it looks like the good guys are using suppressors. Well, at least we'll be able to tell them apart. A couple of rounds ricocheted of the top of the bench and I pushed Kelly down with one hand and tried to reach my golf bag and pull it over to me. I left four clubs in my trunk to make room for the Smith and Wesson semiautomatic tactical rifle with a magazine the held thirty 223 caliber rounds, and a couple of extra mags in my side pocket. I was hunkered down keeping Kelly under the heavy cement bench and I caught a glimpse of a muzzle flash from the roof. I removed the ear bud and clear mouth piece from Kelly's ear and put it in mine.

"Hey! Hey! Anybody hear me?" I asked.

"Who is this?" a voice came loud into my ear.

"This is Rockland Reese. I have Billy Kelly here and we're trapped on the far end of the driving range and he's down. I repeat...he's down. There's a shooter on the roof over the south end of the clubhouse."

"Yes Mr. Reese, we know where you are and we have agents breaching the roof of the clubhouse as we speak. Just keep your head down."

I heard a couple of shots and then the line went dead. Then I heard another voice come on, "Agent down, Agent down, in the parking lot!"

Another voice said, "Damn it, someone shoot that son of a bitch."

I slammed a round home into the chamber and flipped the safety off and took aim at the roof. A head popped up and I squeezed the trigger smoothly. The rifle jerked slightly and I saw the head rise up briefly then fall backwards. Then all hell broke loose, bullets began to hit all around me. I pushed Kelly farther under the bench and yelled into the mouth piece. "What the hell is going on? Where is my support?"

"Just stay calm Mr. Reese, we're all around you and closing in."

"Well, damn it! Shoot somebody then."

Blood was running down my right arm and I was really getting pissed. A bullet grazed my left calf and it hurt like hell, then I heard Kelly moan.

"Are you awake?"

"Yeah, I'm good," he said.

"Okay, then watch yourself because it's getting crazy out here. You need to stay under there until somebody comes for you, I gotta go."

I tried to stand but fell back to the ground just as two or three bullets hit around me, blood now gushing down my leg. I guess it was more than just a graze. It looked to me like some of the rounds were coming from the far end of the driving range, east of the property.

"Has anyone got eyes on Martinez?" I asked.

No answer.

"Is anyone still out there?"

A voice came back, "Yeah, we're here, at least some of us."

"How many are we up against?" I asked. "Where's Martinez?"

"He's in the restaurant and he has a couple of hostages."

"What? What the hell are you idiots running out there, a party for the Mafia, or what?"

Silence again.

"Who's second in command here?" I asked.

"It was Berry Clark, but he's down in the parking lot."

"Well who the hell is next?" I yelled.

"Rocco, are you there?"

"Dan! Is that you? Thank God. Will you take over this mess and get me out of here?"

I crawled low against the fence that ran behind the benches at the range, toward the clubhouse. I heard shots fired up on the roof without silencers; the bad guys. I crawled some more in the direction of the main building, the concrete tables and benches on the patio provided me some cover as I moved.

"Roc, this is Dan. Just stay where you are, will you please. You're gonna get shot."

"I've already been shot, twice! I'm pissed and I'm gonna get Martinez if it's the last thing I do. Are you taking care of those guys on the roof of the club?"

"...already on it," Dan said.

"What about the guys to the east?"

"My guys put them down about thirty seconds ago. We are scanning the property now for any others, but I think it's just inside."

I heard pistol shots from inside the club house and saw muzzle flashes. I made my way toward a door that opened out to the patio and hoped it was unlocked. I stood up and tugged on the door handle but it didn't give.

"Crap!"

I brought my rifle up just as the door exploded and dark shaded glass hit me all over. My Ray-Bans kept me from getting glass in my eyes, but I was bleeding from hundreds of small cuts and my shirt and pants were in shreds. I dropped to the ground again and belly crawled back to the closest cement bench as I called for Dan.

"Hey Buddy! Are you there?"

"Yeah Roc, I'm here.

"What the hell is going on in there?"

"Uh...Lucy's in there, Roc."

"What? Dan, are you kidding me?"

"One of those young FED kids was watching her and she kicked him in the nuts."

"Damn it! Dan, I'm going in."

"I'm about thirty seconds from coming in the front door. Let's get this thing over with before anyone else gets hurt."

"See you inside," and I went silent.

I looked like Satan, completely red covered in blood from head to toe. I could still hear shots inside. I stood and limped over to the door and entered. A quick scan and I saw Juan Martinez with his arms around Lucy using her as a shield, but his back was to me. He was watching for Dan. From his position, Dan would be shot as soon as he enters. I had to get his attention and I couldn't wait any longer. I walked into the room.

"You owe me five grand and a new car, you son of a bitch!

He turned and put Lucy between him and me.

"I'm gonna kill her if you come any closer."

"You do what you have to do, Juan, but one thing is for sure, you are a dead man.

"I'm not dead yet, my friend."

"All of your men are dead or dying, and you're the only one left standing, and I'm going to kill you."

I started walking toward him. I was about 30 feet from him when he lowered his gun from Lucy's head and squeezed of three shot in my direction. One whizzed by my left ear, one grazed my side just above my waist band and the third hit me square in the left shoulder making me twist about 45 degrees and then back. Lucy broke loose and dove to her left and I pulled the trigger on the Smith &Wesson assault rifle while I started walking toward Juan. I never stopped squeezing the trigger as I moved forward hitting him once, twice, three times. I kept moving closer and firing until my magazine was completely empty and I was standing over him. He had twenty seven 223 caliber bullets in him almost all in his chest, and two that I made sure hit him between the eyes. A double tap, just to make sure there was no way the bastard was walking away from this.

Then the pain hit me; a bullet crease in my left side, a hole in my left calf, my right bicep, my left shoulder, and a thousand shreds of glass in me.

"Damn this hurts," I said out loud but to myself and I sat down on the floor and leaned against a circular table that had been turned over on its side and I closed my eyes.

'Where oh where can my baby be, the Lord took her away from me. She's gone to heaven, so I got to be good so I can see my baby when I leave this world." Last Kiss, J. Frank Wilson & the Cavaliers 1964.'

Hole 16
Hunting My Bird

I woke up in room 319 with a really good view of the Pacific. At least it would have been if Lucy hadn't been standing between me and the window, either way, a great view. San Diego General Hospital; not bad as far as hospitals go, but I hate them all.

"Hey girl, can I get out of here? I really need a drink."

"Sure," she said with a cute smile on her face that quickly turned into a very mean and ugly frown. "You can leave, if you live, you son of a...."

"This may be the most clothes I've seen you wear since I've known you. Can't even get close to seeing through that sweatshirt," I interrupted trying to change the subject.

"Oh shut up, you crazy old bastard."

"What! Are you telling me, the honeymoon is over?"

"Not if you live, but that's kind of questionable at the moment. You really scared me, Roc." Lucy replied.

"It's just a couple of small holes," I said.

"Yes...and over 300 pieces of glass. That is, if they got them all."

"You didn't happen to bring my flask with you, did you," I asked.

"Are you a psychic?" Lucy said. "How did you know?"

"Just wishful thinking, I guess. And I could really use some of that good pot."

"You'll have to wait till tomorrow for that."

She slept on half of my hospital bed with her head on my right shoulder and I watched TV and sipped on Crown most of the night. I finished off the bottle at about 2am, and just like clockwork, the pain started returning about an hour later. I grabbed the remote on the side of the bed and called for a nurse. While I was waiting for her to come in I realized that Lucy, who was now sound asleep on my right arm, left the empty bottle of crown on the bedside table, just out of reach.

"Crap!" I said in a loud whisper just as the nurse entered.

"Yeah, what can I do for you, Hun?" she asked.

She was new and had just come on shift. She picked up my chart and began reading.

"I could use some serious pain meds, since I'm out of Crown."

I thought it might be best just to admit the alcohol since she is obviously staring right at the empty bottle.

"Mr. Reese! We do not allow alcohol in this...," she yelled and then stopped all of a sudden.

"Roc Reese? I'm so sorry. I didn't realize it was you. Four bullet wounds and over 300 glass extractions? What can I get for you? Anything you need Rocco. Can I call you Rocco?"

"I'm a little out of it, but I know I would have remembered an Angel of Mercy like you."

"We have never met, but I know your work. The lady in the restaurant that was hit in the leg by a stray bullet, she was my sister. They brought her here and she told me all about how you rushed over and helped her even though you were being shot at. I can't tell you how much that meant to her. Then I saw you on the Telly. You are a true hero. What can I get for you?"

"A couple of hypodermics of cocaine should do for a start," I said.

"That shouldn't be a problem," she said and left on a mission.

"Hey, can you shut the hell up over there? Don't you know what time it is?"

"Kelly, is that you? Are you telling me the good old US of A can't even afford a private room for one of their best?"

"I usually don't mind sharing," he said.

"I was talking about me," I said trying to get a laugh.

My nurse walked back into the room with a couple of needles; one in her hand and one in her pocket.

"This one's from your doctor," she said as she injected one into my IV. "...and this one's from me, our little secret." She injected the second syringe into my left arm and wiped the spot with a wet towel.

"Hey! What about me? I'm in pain too."

"Sorry Mr. Kelly," she said. "I just gave yours to the Rock, but I'll see if I can find you some Tylenol or Advil or something after I finish making my rounds."

"What! You do know I've been shot, don't you?"

"Yes, of course, but only once," she said with a smile in her voice.

Kelly's bride from Scottsdale, Arizona came into the room round 10 AM and she was adorable, in her own way. We had the curtain between the beds drawn back and I said, "Kelly! Shame on you she's a very beautiful lady and I don't see a broom,"

I winked at her and he turned red. She and Lucy took to each other in a heartbeat and they left to go get a cup of coffee when she found that his pride was hurt more than anything else.

It was three weeks later and we were on I-10 heading east out of San Bernardino towards Scottsdale to do some interior designing at the Kelly residence and Lucy loved driving the big Lexus. It's like floating on a cloud, if you can call 105 mph floating. She only got stopped twice but used the story about her grandfather going to M.D. Anderson for treatment along with her already short skirt hiked up even higher than normal and the California and Arizona Highway Patrol didn't have a chance. My scars were still very obvious and made me look even older than my 60 years. I coughed a couple of times and the Arizona guy even offered to give us an escort the rest of the way. I don't believe he had all of the alluring Miss Barnes that he wanted yet.

We made the 364 miles in less than four hours and we were parked in the Kelly's driveway at two in the afternoon. Out north of town in the Boulders, in a very nice 4000 square foot ranch style hacienda about a block away from the golf course.

"You should see the course, Rocco. I have only been on it a couple of times, but I hear it's one of the best in the southwest."

"Take my word for it, Kelly, it is. I've played it many times. In fact, I have a very good friend that lives on the third hole."

"We can go out tomorrow if you like, while the girls shop or whatever."

Lucy looked at him with a scowl.

"What?" he asked.

"You're not going near a golf course, without me."

I just shrugged, "You ain't real smart are you, son?" and we laughed.

The girls were up and gone by seven, and Kelly and I had waffles, eggs and really good coffee at the grill. Gary Moore, my golf buddy that I've known since our days in the Coast Guard, met us and we told stories that kept Kelly laughing for over two hours. We were getting ready to leave when the staff came out from the clubhouse, the golf shop, the kitchen and everywhere else and began to clap.

"What'd you do, tell them it's my Birthday or something?" I asked as I turned to Kelly.

The general manager came up to me, shook my hand and presented me with a complimentary membership to the Boulders Golf Club and Spa. Everyone just continued clapping and cheering.

"What's this all about?" I asked Kelly again.

"Well, Sir, you're kind of a legend around here. After your crash in La Jolla, then your exploits down in Mexico and finally the battle at the driving range; wiping out that Martinez cartel, you are a hero. We don't have much use for drug lords around here," said the manager.

"People keep using that word. I was just trying to stay alive. But...thank you. Thank you very much."

'Somewhere, beyond the sea, somewhere waiting for me, my lover stands on golden sands...Bobby Darin 1960'

We played that afternoon and the girls looked amazing. I don't know if they hit any golf shots or not, and I really don't care. It was all I could do to break 80. I still felt pretty rough and watching Miss Lucy and Kelly's wife prance around in their skimpy golf outfits kept me from overdoing it. We stayed two nights with the Kelly's then moved to a casita at the club and spent two more days and nights pampering ourselves; Jacuzzi's, massages, lots of golf, great dining and drinking. We sat on the patio every night and drank good whisky and every once in a while we would roll a little of Juan Martinez's Best. My body was making a remarkable recovery.

I drove on the way home and kept the cruise control on 84. State police went by and just waved. Around San Bernardino, a cop did pull up behind me, and after following for a couple miles, finally flashed his lights. I think just because he had heard about Lucy through the grapevine.

"Be good, Roc. I mean it," Lucy said as we came to a stop.

"License and registration," he said as he bent over to look in the window.

"Sure, what seems to be the problem, officer?" I said trying to be on my best behavior.

"You were going a little fast back there. Where are you headed in such a hurry?"

"My fifth wife ran off with a State Trooper and I was afraid you were bringing her back." I couldn't help myself. It just fit. Lucy was trying to be mad at me, but was smiling. I knew she was laughing on the inside.

"You drinking?" he asked.

"You buying?" I asked realizing that I should stop. Lucy sputtered trying not to laugh as she looked away from him.

"Do I smell pot?" he asked.

"Do I smell donuts?" I asked as Lucy was now laughing out loud.

"That's it buddy. Out of the car."

"Did you see my license, officer?"

He looked down into his hand and along with my license he saw the business card of Special Agent Billy Kelly, Federal Bureau of Investigations. I also had given him the business card of Chief Dan Brown, San Diego Police Department. I always keep these cards with my license.

"I'm sorry officer. I was just joking around. I thought you were too. I sure didn't mean any disrespect," I said in my best humble voice.

"Mr. Reese, I heard what you went through over in San Diego. I wish I could have been there to help. You all drive safe."

He handed my license and cards back to me through the window and walked back to his car. As I went to put them away in my wallet, I noticed a new card; Sergeant Andrew Daniels, San Bernardino Police Department.

"I guess we have a new friend."

Lucy was just coming out of her laughing fit as she pulled my head over and kissed the top of it.

"You crazy old man," she said.

We spent that night at my condo and ordered in fresh seafood and strawberry cheese cake from Jaxons. The ocean was even more beautiful than the last time we were here, and so was Miss Lucy Barnes.

I called JJ.

"Hey, you about ready to tee it up? You really need to see my partner swing a club."

"Yeah, but does she play any golf," he joked.

"You're quick. I don't remember you being that smart."

"Let me call you back in a couple of minutes."

My phone rang a few minutes later.

"I got us setup as a six some at the San Luis Club at ten tomorrow."

"What's the set up?"

"We can play the back first and then have lunch then we'll have the front all to ourselves. A grand a stick okay?"

"You're a good man, JJ. See you around 9:30 at the club."

"What does that mean?" Lucy asked.

"You don't need to worry about it. I got this."

"I'm not worried. I just want to learn what we are doing."

"You're right. You need to know this. A grand a stick means each player is playing for a thousand dollars per bet. So, if we win two bets on the front nine, each one of the other team members owes $2000, and so on and so forth.

Lucy was very nervous, this being her first game for money. Except against me, which she never paid...at least not in cash.

"Just relax...concentrate on hitting your target and keeping your shorts rolled up and we'll have a few extra bucks in our pockets and have a great time doing it."

We pulled up next to JJ's Jaguar and he whistled.

"Wow! Is that new?"

"No. She's 32," I said.

Lucy caught me with a right in the ribs that almost knocked the wind out of me.

"I was talking about the car?" he said.

"Haven't you seen it? It's just a little gift from Neil."

"That's quite a gift," JJ said. "I looked at those, and I know what they run."

"Yeah...and worth every penny...wait, that doesn't even make sense, does it? Worth every dollar," I said. "Who are we playing?"

"Remember the good Dr. Billy Wilson that we let beat us out of $200 a couple of years ago in hopes he'd play us for a bigger pot?"

"Yeah, I do."

"Well, he always wanted to. He could just never make the dates come out right. Now he's retired and he has all the time and money in the world. And he still thinks he can beat us."

"Way to go my friend. Let's do this dance."

I told Lucy not to worry about anything that's said. "Just play your game and hit every shot as good as you can. You hear?"

"Yes, Daddy!"

"Better make it Partner. We may want to get at these guys again someday."

We all drove to the tenth tee; four golf carts and six players. I hate playing sixes or even fives. I'm a very fast player and if you get one or two players that have a problem committing, it can take five or six hours to play a round. If I'm on the course over three and a half, it's stops being fun.

We made all the introductions and I remembered Doc Wilson. I kind of liked him and now that he was retired he seemed even more relaxed and fun to be around. His two other partners were friendly enough, although they didn't warm up to Lucy at first. The male golfer is a unique specimen. We hate to be inconvenienced and we don't want to have to compensate or play down to a woman's inferior ability; that is unless there is something in it for us. Lucy was wearing her light pull-away Reebok pants and a long-sleeved windbreaker until she got out of the cart. She stretched tall removing her windbreaker high above her head while standing on the tee box and looking down the fairway, completely ignoring all the men standing there with their mouths hung open. Then she began unbuttoning the snaps on the sides of her pants, all the way down her long, unbent legs revealing her short shorts. Her legs were perfect, and even I had to do a double take to see if she was wearing high heels. The last button on her right ankle didn't release and she reached down to unsnap it, bending only at the waist. I don't know how she planned that, but it worked beautifully. The guys were in love: one of them dropped his driver and another one actually had to sit down. I thought he was going to have a heart attack. There was even a catcall from the thirteenth fairway behind us. I couldn't have planned it any better. We played from the senior tees, which were also the ladies and my plan was was coming together. Usually when a senior hits his tee shot he goes back and sits in his cart to conserve energy, but when Lucy was hitting last, I noticed they all stayed on the tee box to see the show, and she didn't disappoint. She was beating all but one of our opponents but they didn't seem to mind, and JJ and I were taking real good care of the bets. After the front nine, we were up 3K and these guys couldn't wait to get out and see the rest of the show and donate to the cause; 'cause we wanted their do re mi.

The back nine went even better than the front, at least for our team. They were pressing and talking to Lucy and having the time of their old lives. I think one of them even asked her for a date. Oh well, can't say I blame him. At the end of the round we were up 7 bets.

We sat around a large table on the patio and had cocktails and chips and salsa. I picked up the bar tab, $223 with the tip and it was my pleasure to pay it. They wanted to play us again and I told JJ to set it up.

On the ride home Lucy asked how we did, and I pulled a stack of 100's from my shirt pocket and handed them to her. She counted them out loud just for fun.

"This is a lot of money, Roc! How much is mine?"

"We're partners aren't we?"

She nodded her head.

"Then it's all yours."

"Wait, this can't be right," she said.

"No, it's right. Weren't you paying attention?"

"No, you told me just to relax and play golf. That's what I did. But there's $7,000 here."

"Yeah, you did. 76; a really good score, Lady."

"What did you shoot?" she asked.

"I don't know, 71 or something." Actually I knew exactly what I shot, I always knew.

"You mean these old gentlemen gave us $7,000 apiece and they're not upset?"

"That's exactly what I mean, Love."

"How can that be, Roc?"

"Well, these guys will go to Vegas and drop 30 or 40K in an evening on the craps or poker tables. And they won't have anything like the fun they had today; fresh air, good company and a stage show you couldn't buy in Vegas at any price."

"And they want to do it again?"

"Yep."

My phone rang and I pushed the button on the steering wheel and said, "This is Roc."

"Hey Roc, it's Neil. Where are you?"

"On my way home from San Louie, what's up?"

"Can you meet me at Jerry's for a cup of coffee?"

"Sure, I'm about fifteen minutes out."

"Great, see you there."

We walked in and every head in the place turned and looked at Lucy. Jerry came over personally and held a chair for her. I think he even offered her a job.

"Looks like you're about all healed," Neil said.

"Yeah, just about. Had a pretty good nurse."

"I can only imagine, she's enough to make me go straight," he said. "Say, didn't you say you always wanted a Vet and never got around to getting one?"

"Yeah," I said with a little trepidation in my voice.

"Do you like convertibles?" he asked.

"Sure, nothing like a rag top on the coast."

"Hope you like red," and he tossed me the remote to a 2014.

"I can't take this. I can't afford to register all these cars or pay the insurance."

He looked me in the eye and said, "Maybe this will help." He handed me a check for one hundred thousand dollars.

"Neil, are you nuts? You've already paid me way more than enough."

"Are you crazy, old man? You almost got killed cleaning up my dad's mess. And I know the world is a better place without Juan Martinez around, although Martina may not agree."

"Uh, yeah...how did you know her name?"

"Oh, I guess I saw it on the news. Anyway, I've noticed you have a lot more cars than you have room for, so I'd like to make you a proposition.

"What's that?"

"I thought you guys could move into my dad's place so you can spread out a little; no charge of course."

"But I like living on the beach."

"So keep your condo as well. You probably didn't know that I own the complex you live in, at least most of it. You own yours. The deed will be delivered to you in a few days."

I just sat there looking confused.

"Oh, come on Roc. You're a better detective than that."

"I'm not a detective, I'm a golfer. I play golf for a living, I always have, I always will. That's all I do!"

"I really like you, Roc and I may need a dad to talk with from time to time. You saved me from going through all kinds of hell to get the estate settled; I only thought I was rich before. I'm not sure I even know yet how many hundreds of millions I have now, and it's all because of you. So don't ever tell me it's too much again, got it?"

"Yeah, I got it, I guess." I said somewhat dumbfounded.

We left Neil drinking coffee and Jerry gazing at Lucy's shapely behind as we walked out, headed to San Diego.

"You want to see the new digs?" I asked.

"How big is it?" she asked.

"As close as I can tell, about 80."

"80 what?"

"80,000 square feet."

"Shut Up!"

"Okay, prepare yourself for one hell of a ride."

Hole 17
Bottom of the Cup

We drove up the quarter mile driveway and I couldn't get her to close her mouth.

"Shut Up! Just this morning I was living in an 1100 square foot apartment and now we have an 80,000 square foot mansion? Well, you have a mansion."

"Hey, we're partners. Besides, what would I do in this place without you? I wouldn't have anyone to putt with."

"To putt with?" she asked.

"Yeah, there's an indoor pitch and putt course, I'm just not sure I can remember where it is. And if I get tired of you, I can always hide in there till I die; you'll never find me.

She smacked my right shoulder and it felt kind of good for a change. The sun was setting by the time we finished the tour. Well, not finished, but done.

“Well, where do you want to stay tonight, your place, my place or our place?”

“Oh, I hate making decisions, you pick.”

“Well then, I pick our place.”

“Perfect,” she said. “Do we need a toothbrush?”

“Don’t quote me on this, but I’m pretty sure we can find a new toothbrush or two around here.”

We walked upstairs to check out the master bedroom and when we opened the door Lucy just sat down crossed legged on the floor.

“Can you believe this? We could put our apartments in each corner and still have room for a basketball court in here.”

“That’s downstairs,” I said.

“What’s downstairs?”

“...the indoor basketball court, alongside the pool.”

“There’s an indoor pool?”

“...and an outdoor one as well.”

“Damn!” she said.

Lucy didn't cuss that often. She once told me that ladies don’t talk like that. I guess this was just too overwhelming.

The bed was custom made about three feet longer and five feet wider than a California King, She was bouncing around and squealing.

“Where would you even get sheets for something like this?”

I opened a cabinet that went from the floor all the way to the top of the fourteen foot ceiling.

“Right here, I guess.”

There had to be thirty sets of sheets and pillowcases in every color imaginable and at least a dozen spreads.

"I wonder who makes the bed. I don't think I can even lift the covers."

"I guess we'll have to hire a bed guy," she said as she giggled. "Come over here, you big hunk and help me figure out how to fire up the TV."

There was a remote about the size of a laptop. I pushed a button at the top and the fireplace came on.

"Whoops."

I pushed it again to shut it off. I pushed another and the curtains opened with the most incredible view of the Pacific Ocean.

"Whoops."

I pushed it again to close them.

"No, leave it, and put the fireplace back on," Lucy said.

I pressed another and a disco ball came down from the ceiling and lit up and started turning over the massive bed. Lucy and I both said, "Whoops."

I pressed that button again and the ball retracted into the ceiling. I pressed another and nothing happened. We both sat there for a second, looking around the room to see what might have changed. Then all of a sudden we could smell the soft scent of vanilla, and lavender, and fresh cotton, and lemon, and coffee...I'm not sure what it was, but it smelled so great.

"How many more button are their?" Lucy asked.

"Looks like only...about 18 or 20."

"We may want to wait till morning and I find the manual."

“What we really need is a cocktail,” I said.

“You take the back and I’ll take the front,” she said as she jumped up out of the bed.

We looked in drawers, and cabinets and closets and behind armoires.

“I found the bar,” she yelled, and the lights came on as she got close. “What kind of beer do you want?”

“What kind you got?”

“Coors, Bud, Shiner Bock, and a couple more I can't pronounce.”

“Surprise me,” I said.

“Frozen mug?”

“Sure, why not?”

“Would you like a shot to go with it, Sir?” she asked in her best bartender voice.

“Who is this lady and what’s she doing in my bedroom?” I joked.

“It appears you're in need of a wench to serve you, Sire.”

“We’ll if that be the case, then I shall make do with ye, till I can find a suitable maiden that can keep a civil tongue in her mouth.”

“I’m truly sorry, Sire. Maybe I can make it up to you by putting my uncivil tongue in your mouth.”

She slipped out of her golf shorts and top and came to me naked with a tray of drinks and glasses.

About thirty minutes later I pushed a button on the remote and a TV dropped down from the ceiling. It was the width of the bed and about five feet high. I pushed another button and the screen came to life.

“What would you like to watch?” I asked.

“It really doesn’t matter to me,” she replied.

"Have we eaten lately? I'm getting kind of hungry. Maybe we should go down and raid the fridge."

"Do you suppose we're alone?" she asked.

"I think so, but even if we're not, it would take someone a week to find us."

Lucy jumped down from the bed and headed down the hall with her amazing behind wiggling and glowing from the concealed lighting. We started going through the largest refrigerator I had ever seen. It was full of Salami, Swiss cheese, sliced prime rib, ham, cherry tomatoes and fresh California strawberries. We looked in one of the pantries and found crackers of all kinds. I heard the speakers come on, 'Thank the Lord for the night time,' by Neil Diamond 1967, or maybe it was just in my head. No matter.

The next morning we looked around the top floor and found closets and rooms filled with new clothes and shoes; men's and women's. There were a half a dozen bedrooms, each with their own bath and all the rooms completely decorated and ready to live in, though it looked like no one had ever slept in them. Every bathroom had its own stash of drugs, pot and of course, toiletries.

We walked into the pool naked and unafraid.

"Is this just the best way to wake in the morning or what?" Lucy asked.

We stepped out, grabbed a club and hit a couple of balls to an Astroturf green about 90 yards away. Watching Lucy hit golf shots in the nude was just about the most exciting thing I have ever experienced.

"I may have just discovered a new venture for us. Can I video this?" I asked.

"In your dreams!" she replied.

Just then the doorbell rang throughout the whole pool and recreation area. I grabbed a couple of very large bath towels and threw one to Lucy.

"I wonder where the intercom is," I said to Lucy.

A voice came over the speakers and filled the house, "There's a panel at every door."

"Who's there?" I asked pushing the green talk button.

"It's Maggie, the housekeeper. Just push the button with a key on it, then push the kitchen outside door, and I'll be in."

We found an elevator over in the corner and we took it back up to the second floor and made our way back to the master bedroom to shower and get dressed.

"Let's go to my place and pick up your car, get some clothes and you can get some necessities at your place. Then we'll meet back here," I said.

We took the red Vet and it was so cool. I missed the turn off to my place and kept heading north on the 5 for about 25 miles. Lucy didn't say a word; she just sat back in the leather bucket seat with her eyes closed, the wind moving her long blond hair around her lovely face.

"Roc, Is this a dream?" she asked. "It seems like just yesterday you were sitting in Jaxon's having shrimp and beer, I was serving you and we were just normal people."

"Yeah, I've been thinking about that. You know, they say if it seems too good to be true, it probably is. Besides, something is just not right."

"What do you mean?"

“Why did Martinez take Ray out quietly with a sniper, but then have no problem trying to kill me in public? Old Juan doesn’t really strike me as the kind of guy that hires a sniper. If he wants you dead, one of his guys walks up and kills you. Damn the consequences.”

“You don’t think Juan wanted to kill Ray?”

“No, this was an afterthought. And how did Neil know who Martina is? He would have no reason to know her...and he seems to be very free with his money when it comes to us. I’d like to think he see’s me as a father figure but he’s too old and too rich to need a daddy, don’t you think? Besides, he has Bob Carlson...working with him? That’s it. They never planned on me figuring this out. We were never supposed to go down to Mexico, and we were sure never supposed to come back. No, it makes a lot more sense that he’s paying us off and wanting us to stop digging.”

“We can’t do that? I mean, Ray was not a good guy. Can’t we just leave it alone?” she asked.

“Sweetheart, you know we can’t. Bob and Neil can never be sure how much we know. No, when things calm down, we’ll be lying on the driveway just like Ray.”

“So, what do we do?”

“Just stay alert. I bet this car has GPS and they know exactly where we are. It may even be bugged. And I’ll bet there’s a whole lot more going on at the mansion then we are aware of.

“Like what?” she asked.

“The more I think about it the more I believe we put on a hell of a show for someone since we’ve been there.”

"That makes me feel really creepy and dirty," she said.

"I don't know about all that, but it does really piss me off, and if I'm correct, someone is in for one hell of an ass whippin'. A lot of good cops and Feds died because of this. Just keep alert. I need to check out our places really close. They've had plenty of time to bug them in the last month or so. I need to get in touch with Kelly and Chief Dan and tell them what we think is going on."

I was going to drop Lucy at my place to get her car but then thought twice. I warned her not to say anything about this to anyone and not to make any phone calls from her apartment. I knew I couldn't drive the Vet or Ray's Lexus, but I sat there for just a second and tried to think of a way to make either one of those happen. Yeah, they were that nice. They might have bugged Lucy's new car, but they would never waste time and effort bugging my car when they know I would drive a nicer one. I put the new Vet in the garage, got the key for my old wreck and we headed to the SDPD to meet Dan.

We put Billy Kelly on the speaker in Dan's office as I ran threw the scenario that was bubbling in my brain.

By the time we were finished, I had them both persuaded that I was on to something. Billy was already putting a team together to sweep all the residences and vehicles and start doing more background checks on Neil and Robert, the new partners. Well, not as new as Lucy and I, but nonetheless, pretty new.

"Are we moving backwards?" Lucy asked. "All of a sudden we're driving a seven year old car and heading for a cheap motel."

"Okay, okay. We'll get a very expensive motel."

"Thank you. We made fourteen thousand dollars yesterday, not counting what Neil gave you. Besides, I've never been a cheap motel kind of girl."

"I never thought you were, Sweetheart."

The San Diego Wild Surf is on the beach and is $1300 a night. Of course that includes towels and bath robes, and a complimentary breakfast, so that makes all the difference. It wouldn't take long to eat up fourteen thousand dollars at this rate, good thing I don't have a mortgage or any car payments.

"What do you want to do about dinner?" she asked.

"Eat it, I guess."

"Very funny..."

"Well, the cafe down stairs looks tolerable." I said.

"Cafe? Did you look at the menu? There's nothing under three hundred bucks."

"Does that include ice water?" I asked.

"You better get us some golf matches if we're going to stay here very long."

"Hey Lover, you're the one that said no cheap motels."

"Isn't there a happy medium somewhere?"

"Maybe, but let's enjoy this while we're here."

Our sliding glass door opened to the beach with a small patio, a table and four chairs and maybe twenty steps to the water. It turned dark and we had cocktails on the lanai and decided to have room service for dinner; three dozen oysters on the half shell, a very fresh garden salad with the best blue cheese dressing I've ever had, and Lobster Mac and Cheese with an incredible Chardonnay that the hotel sommelier recommended.

"Do you want dessert?" I asked.

"Let's wait and see if the oysters kick in," she said with a smile.

My cell phone rang before we even had the coffee brewing.

"This is Roc," I said in my very unfriendly morning voice.

"Hey Roc, it's Billy. You were absolutely dead on, no pun intended. Everything you own and some things you don't; all bugged, with some very sophisticated listening and video equipment."

"Are your guys all done?" I asked.

"We still have to get Lucy's car and your Lexus but they should be through in the next hour or so. I'd buy you guys coffee in the restaurant, but I know how expensive that place is and I only have three hundred in cash with me," he said laughing.

"Come on to the room, the pot's on."

"On my way."

We drank joe and talked about the bugs while Lucy got herself ready for the day. Just as I suspected, everything pointed directly at my son, Neil Benson and his partner Robert Carlson.

"You handle Bob, 'cause I'm going to shoot Neil in the kneecaps just for fun."

"Same rules apply, Roc. Self-defense is one thing but I can't sanction a hit. I'd lose my job and probably end up in jail, myself."

"Don't worry, Kelly. I won't let you get in trouble for this. Besides, anytime I get really pissed off and shoot somebody in the kneecaps just before I kill them, it's always self-defense."

We got the all clear from Kelly's boys. Lucy's car was hot, but sure enough, they didn't bother mine; criminals are so predictable, especially dumb ones. We checked out of the money pit on the beach and headed back to my condo and straight into some beachwear. Mentally, I was ready for, and in need of some peace and quiet. We carried the two-man, twelve foot kayak down to the beach; it seemed to be tougher than usual. Maybe I was weaker, maybe I was getting older, or maybe it was the two automatic rifles we had over our shoulder and under towels to hide them from the public. I wasn't going to be caught out there again, unprepared. We put in and headed out to deep water. We paddled hard and skimmed across the water at a really good pace. Lucy was feeling trapped and had the same need to get some fresh air and exercise that I did. We went to the two mile mark, then we headed back without slowing and we completed the four mile trek in record time. Lucy wasn't even breathing hard but my 60 year old body was shaking some and I was sucking air a little harder than I would have liked. I'm not sure if my association with my new partner was getting me in better shape or killing me, but there were definitely some changes taking place in my body.

"Should I start to worry?" Lucy asked.

"Nah, I'll probably be shot before my heart attack gets here."

We showered and as we got dressed I asked Lucy what she would like to do.

"I would love to play a few holes, and then get drunk and forget about being a target for a while."

"Well, we can sure play some, and have a great dinner. I'll even make sure we take the edge off, but Sweetie, we can't relax just yet."

"You asked me what I wanted, not what I thought we should do," she stated.

I got a couple of lobs and a 14 ounce filet from the freezer and placed them in the sink under cold water. We loaded our clubs and went to a small, out of the way par three course up the coast a couple of miles. We split a small bucket and then played nine holes. I shot even par 27 and Lucy shot two over 29. Damn! She really is coming along. We got back to my place and I finished defrosting the filet and lobs in the microwave while I fired up the grill.

Lucy poured us a really strong Crown on the rocks and then another as I charred the steak and grilled the lobster slathering them both with garlic drawn butter and that was it. We decided we didn't want a vegetable or salad or bread or anything. We sat on the patio and ate perfectly grilled meat. The sommelier at the hotel told me that you should have a good Chardonnay with lobster, but my filet was demanding a good Cabernet, so we decided to have both. We fell asleep on the sofa in each others arms watching Fox News. About three in the morning I thought about carrying Lucy into the bedroom. As I bent down to pick her up I realized what a dumb idea that was, so I woke her up and led her to bed.

My phone rang while I was on my second cup of coffee and Lucy was in the shower. It was Kelly, and Dan on the line as well.

"A conference call...this must be important."

"Yeah, well, that friend of yours, Neil? Turns out he's not gay and we think he was the shooter that took down Ray Benson."

"He shot his own dad? That pretty cold."

"That means he'll have no problem putting a long distance slug in you."

"Well, I'm gonna leave this thing in both your capable hands, and we're going to work; at Torrey Pines."

Hole 18
Settling the Bets

The regular boys at Torrey Pines weren't too excited to see a woman, but no one said anything and they all wanted to play her for a grand with a two-down auto. Lucy and I and three of the regulars played in the first group, I wanted to make sure that everyone could see Lucy almost all the time. I had already heard some comments and I knew the fix was in.

"Don't get in a hurry and take a couple of extra practice swings. Let's keep them waiting just enough to make them watch and to annoy them all at the same time."

Since we were riding together, I had the opportunity to coach her and she listened to everything I had to say. Her total take for the day was over thirty grand. She had a long drive, three skins, and two birdies and a couple of polies that they sure didn't expect. She halved one of her bets and won the other four.

"Don't think we don't know what you're doing here, Roc. Bringing out that damn movie star to keep all us old pecker woods excited and confused," a retired business executive said. "...and me for one, I really enjoyed it. Besides she swings a pretty good stick," and we laughed.

On the way back to town I tossed her our winnings and she counted it.

"Roc, do you know how much money we have here?"

I played dumb, "No, haven't had time to count it up yet."

"$48,000," she said.

"Actually, forty nine. I kept a grand for gas money," and she busted out laughing.

"Do these guys do this every week?"

"Twice a week," I replied.

"And do you beat them like this every time?"

"Sometimes a little more, sometimes a little less. They're my regular job, the other games are bonuses."

"So you took me as a partner?" she said.

"Hey! Just wait a minute, you asked me to be your partner," I said.

"Yeah, but I thought we were just gonna decorate some houses and make a couple of grand a week."

"We still can, if that's what you want to do. I want you to be happy, Girl."

"Shut Up! Is this legal? I mean, I don't want you to die in jail."

"Oh, thanks. Where do you want me to die?" I asked. "Yes, it's perfectly legal. Maybe not very ethical, but completely legal, and now they're going to be calling, wanting to play with you. I'll just be along to make sure we don't lose."

"And what about JJ? How does he make his money?"

"Well, in this game he's on his own. We don't bet each other, but nobody knows that. And on the other days when we're a team we split everything down the middle, three ways, now that you're here."

"There's something just wrong about this," she said.

"Okay, let me explain it like this...when you were tending bar, didn't you try to get certain customer to leave you a bigger tip by flirting with them?"

"Sure, if I thought they could afford it."

"Right, so when these guys go out to dinner, they leave a $500 tip. When they go to Vegas, they play in the private rooms for 50 to a 100 thousand. Do you know why?"

"No, why?" she asked.

"...because they have so much money that their hearts don't start beating until they gamble for high stakes. These guys would pay thirty or forty grand just to ride around in a golf car and watch you play."

"Yeah, right."

"Seriously, they told me so today. You have only played three rounds of golf and you're a legend in this town already."

On our way back into town I stopped by the bank and deposited the hundred thousand from Neil. I was curious to see if the check was still going to be good. Good as gold. When we got back to my place the mail had come and the titles for the new LS and the Vet were in my box. We drove over to the motor vehicle department and registered them.

"If this all goes pear shaped, at least I'll have this done and in my name," I said and Lucy agreed.

"Close to 5pm. What's your pleasure, my lady?"

"You know what I would really like to do? Get the Vet, drive up to Oceanside and have some fish and chips on the pier. I have been thinking about that ever since we were there."

The evening air was starting to chill a little but the heater kept us toasty. The wind blowing through our hair was amazing...okay, through her hair. It was just bouncing of my head so I put on an Angels cap. We watched the seagulls float around above us and we would toss them French fries just to watch them grab it out of the air, amazing creatures. On the way home my cell rang and Kelly's voice came over the speakers.

"Roc, they're on the move and they're looking for you. They've been by your place and by Lucy's too, and up to the mansion a couple of times. I guess they think you're the last of the loose ends."

"How many are we looking at, Kelly?"

"There's just two, the same car keeps pulling up at each place. We haven't been able to get a good look at their faces, but I imagine we are down to Bob and Neil. I could pre-empt this whole thing and just arrest them, probably get them on a weapons charge."

"No. You know they're connected and they'll walk. This has to end today."

"Well, where do you want to end this thing?" Kelly asked.

"How about where it all started...at the house on the hill," I said.

"I figured you would say that. I had my boys place your Smith & Wesson assault rifle with a couple extra clips in the master bedroom. It's under the pillows on the bed. You might want to get to it before the maid cleans in there."

"Thanks, Kelly," we're on our way. I need you and your boys to get out of there. I don't want to scare them off if they see an ambush."

"Okay, we are out...and Roc, I don't know anything about this."

"About what?" I said and the line went dead and Elvis came back on. We were already doing sixty when I stepped on it and the tires squealed. The rear end fishtailed just a hair.

"Wow! Quicker than the Lexus but not as comfortable. But, unless someone shoots the hell out of it, I think I'll hang on to it."

Lucy smiled her approval.

We drove up the quarter mile driveway cautiously, pulled into the last stall and walked through the collection of cars into the house. I looked in all directions and had a pretty good feeling that we were alone. We made it upstairs and I found the assault rifle right where it was supposed to be.

"Check your pistol, and your extra magazine."

I realized that she should not even be here. What was I thinking? I had gotten so used to her being with me that I didn't think this through. I'm used to living my life and dealing with the consequences that come, but now I need to be thinking for her as well.

"You know, you still have time to get out of here."

"No thanks, I'm right where I want to be," she said very nonchalantly.

"Lucy, come on, you've got your whole life ahead of you and mine may end in this big old mansion on the hill. I really do think it's best if you...."

I was interrupted when I got a whiff of smoke.

"Lucy, they're here. You need to start thinking of a way out of here while I find somebody to shoot...and keep your cell phone on silent. I want to be able to contact you but I sure as hell don't want anyone to hear. Got it?"

"Got it, Roc. You be careful."

I looked at the video monitor and caught a quick look as someone passed in front of the camera by one of the doors at the back of the house. I could have sworn it was Bob Carlson with a long gun of some kind in his hands. I put all the cameras up on the screen and it looked like there were about ten figures creeping around the outside. An alarm went off and a light on the screen started to flash; someone had breached the door at the back of the garage. I pushed a button that told me the door from the garage to the house was secured.

"Looks like some of our Mexican friends are involved in this."

"I thought we were done with Martinez," Lucy said.

"This isn't Martinez. This is another cartel, probably smaller than the Martinez one. Good ol' Bob and Neil probably saw an opportunity to take over if they could get Martinez out of the way. Just too greedy to let it go. Greed is a terrible thing and it can get you killed."

I set the rifle in on the bed while I pulled my Glock 19 from my holster and let a 9mm hollow point round slam home. I put another 15 round magazine in my front pocket.

We had some things in our favor. The mansion was brick construction which made it a little more secure than wood or plaster, and there were lots of large rocks built into the facade that would keep bullets from coming through. Another alarm went off and I looked at the screen. A door down in the gym, by the indoor pool was breached and I saw two Mexican looking guys with assault rifles coming through single file. I grabbed my cell and punched the call button twice which brought up and dialed the last call made...Kelly.

"Roc, you okay?"

"Where the hell are you?" I shouted.

"What's going on?"

"What's going on is we have a dozen Mexicans with automatic rifles coming at us from all directions."

"Roc, we're on our way. About seven minutes out."

"Seven minutes? Where the hell did you go, to McDonald's?"

"You're the one that told me to get out of there. I couldn't sit thirty seconds away while a friend of mine executes two people. You know how that would look?"

"Well this is a lot more than two guys, so kick that government Ford in the ass, 'cause seven minutes can be a life time and we might not be alive by the time you get here."

"We're at six and a half now, Roc."

Two bullets slammed through the giant TV screen at the end of the bed and missed my head by inches. I turned just in time to see a tall man get two bullets in his head from my partner that was crouching behind a large leather chair. Her right arm was braced on the armrest and her 9 mm was resting in her left hand, just the way we had practiced. She squeezed of two more rounds and another man went down just as he entered the bedroom. I saw a silhouette at the other door to Lucy's back and I lifted my rifle and squeezed of 6 rounds and a short man with a bandoleer over his shoulder went down to the floor. Another man began yelling and fired into the room without aiming. Stepping to my right to get a better view of the doorway, I let another volley of bullets fly and the second man collapsed. I walked towards the door and put a single shot into the little fat mans head to keep him from coming back to life and shooting Lucy in the back. Then I double tapped the guy just behind him in the head as well.

"Get back over here behind the bed," I yelled at Lucy, and she ran my way and dove onto the giant bed and rolled off the other side for cover.

Smoke was coming from around the closed doors of the elevator and funneling into the bedroom and I was starting to get concerned.

"I guess we won't be leaving that way."

I checked my watch and it had only been three minutes since I hung up with Kelly and I couldn't hear any sirens yet. I put a few rounds through the windows at the back of the room and a few more in the windows at the front. The glass collapsed and the smoke started to filter out of the bedroom.

I heard a familiar voice come over the intercom in the bedroom.

"Mr. Reese, you have a serious problem. You're not going to get out of here."

It was Maggie and she was in the kitchen, according to my screen. I pushed the green button on the intercom.

"Well, Maggie, I got news for you. You and your associates, Bob and Neil aren't either. That siren you hear, that's the FEDs and the SDPD."

"You're bluffing, Mr. Reese. There's nobody coming to help you."

I knew I was bluffing but I hoped it would buy me some time. Right at that moment, I finally heard the faint sound of the FEDs and the SDPD in the background. I turned to Lucy.

"Stay here and do not leave your position until I come back for you, do you understand?"

"Yes, I understand."

I saw Maggie coming up the back stairs on the monitor. I threw my Glock 19 and extra 15 round magazine on the bed and started heading that way. I moved down the hall past the other bedroom doors checking each one as I went. When I got with in view of the stairwell, I crouched down on one knee and waited. I could see that Maggie was being very cautious and had not yet reached the top. I waited until her head came into view, flipped the lever on my rifle from auto to manual and squeezed very smoothly. Two rounds hit the housekeeper in the right temple and she collapsed, falling backward and rolling all the way down to the bottom of the stairs. I checked the video screen and it was clear, at least for the moment. I moved very rapidly down to the first floor and saw a couple of images behind the fake shrubbery in the pool area by the back of the golf green. As I moved down the hall, I heard gun shots from behind me and stopped long enough to make sure no one was tracking me. Feeling confident in my position, I continued on down the hallway. There was a door on my right, just short of the entrance to the recreation area that I hadn't had time to check out yet, so I carefully opened it and looked around. It was a storeroom for sports equipment; sets of golf clubs, basketballs and all kinds of swim gear including flippers, diving tanks, paddle and boogie boards and stuff in new cartons that hadn't even been opened yet. I saw a door that I assumed led to the pool area way down at the far end of the store room. I made my way as quietly as I could and checked the screen on the pad. The two men were still crouching behind the greenery, but I thought I got a good enough look to recognize Neil and Bob.

"All right, assholes. Let's do this dance 'cause I'm getting very tired of screwing with you," I said to myself in a loud whisper.

I switched my rifle back to auto and slipped the mag out and checked it. It was about half full and I had a full one in my front pocket. I decided to put the full one in my gun and have the other for backup. I checked my screen and it looked to be about thirty yards from the door to the bushes with some weight benches and racks of free weights just outside the door and off to the right about fifteen feet. I checked the screen making sure it was clear and belly crawled through the partially opened door to get behind the weights and hopefully use them for cover. I made it without drawing any fire, pulled my rifle level and looked through the scope. This was the first chance

I've had to use it since this whole mess started. The closest image in my view appeared to be Bob Carlson. I put the cross hairs of the scope on his chest and gently squeezed back the trigger. Eight rounds left the barrel and good ol' Bob wiggled, shook and flew backwards into a sand trap landing face down; pretty dead, I would bet. Unfortunately for me, this got Neil's attention and he turned swinging his weapon around with him. Lead started flying my way, bouncing off weights and ricocheting off benches. Basketballs and footballs started flying and going flat, landing all around me as the shelves they came from began to splinter with wood exploding everywhere. I flipped my rifle back to manual and tried to aim, but each time I was about to smooth a round his way, three or four bullets would hit around me. He must have needed to change magazines because there was a break in the fire. Moving quickly, I adjusted my position and sighted him in my scope. I pulled the trigger and he went down behind a bush and out of sight. I wanted to charge him but then I remembered that I was 60 years old. I couldn't run thirty yards on a good day. I continued to look through the scope for a few seconds...no movement. I put my head down and just waited, listening for anything. Nothing...no shots...no movement...nothing.

"Okay, I'm ready to go home and I could use a drink."

I stood and started to make my way toward Neil. Part of me hoped he wasn't dead because I wanted to shoot the bastard a little more, but I sure didn't want him shooting at me. I moved to within ten yards of the spot where he went down just as I was about to relax,

Neil stood with blood streaming down from his left shoulder. He pulled the trigger and three rounds came my way; two just missing my left side and one hitting my forearm. I winced in pain as I pulled the trigger on my rifle. I hit him in the thigh but he didn't go down, just staggered back a couple of steps.

"You son of a bitch! Why didn't you just take the money? Why didn't you just turn your back?" he yelled.

"You and I both know, you were never going to let me just take the money. You proved that the first time you shot at me in the bar."

"How did you know it was me?"

"You told me that your dad was shot at about three-thirty. The cops didn't even know the exact time. You may be smart enough to plan all this with Bob, but you are way too stupid to pull it off."

While I was talking, I flipped my rifle over to automatic. Just then, flames broke out around the ceiling and the roof exploded in smoke and fire. Neil looked up and that was all I needed. I lifted my rifle and pulled the trigger as I moved the rifle from right to left. Bullets strafed across him right at twenty four inches high and took out both his kneecaps, as promised. He collapsed immediately and I took the opportunity to continue firing with six or seven rounds hitting him in the groin area. Then three more hit him in the belly and before I could fire again, a large twelve by twelve timber fell from the ceiling and crushed him into the artificial turf. I looked up and saw a very large hole in the roof and walked over to see him trying to say something. I pointed the muzzle of my rifle at his head, point blank and emptied the rest of my magazine into his face. I dropped my rifle to the ground and walked out the door to the front yard.

I saw Chief Dan coming up the driveway with fire trucks and ambulances behind him. He pulled over quick and got out of his car.

"Roc, You okay?"

"Yeah, never better."

"I thought you might need these guys," he said pointing to the fire truck already raising the ladder to the second floor. "Anything I need to know?"

"Uh...yeah! Be very careful. There's a very pissed off lady up there with a gun. Let me try to contact her, first."

I pulled my cell and pushed the number on the speed dial.

"Yeah," she said choking from the smoke.

The Fire Department is coming through the front window. Don't shoot, got it?"

"Yeah I got it," and she hung up.

"I was sitting on the back of the ambulance being taken care of by a beautiful, young brunette medical tech when Lucy walked up and punched me in the chest almost, taking my breath away.

"Hey! What's that for?" I asked.

"Are you nuts? You old bastard, I watched you on the monitor just walk out there and almost get yourself killed. What were you thinking?"

"I was thinking, I'm hungry, thirsty and tired, and I just want to go home."

She stood there with her mouth open, trembling from anger and trying to collect her thoughts. I didn't want to tell her that I was worried about my partner in the back room and there was no way I was going to let them get to her.

"Well, what would I do without a partner? I haven't learned this business yet."

"Oh...so it's the job you're concerned about?"

She didn't really answer me, but I knew what really bothered her. The fire department had five alarms going and the mansion suffered a large amount of damage, as well as the garage full of burned out cars, including my Vet.

"Well, it was fun while it lasted," I said as we watched my Vet go up in flames and then explode.

Sitting on the patio of my condo that evening, we watched the moon setting over the ocean as we ate lobster tails with avocado halves drizzled in ranch dressing and bacon bits, and of course we enjoyed copious amounts of Crown and some really good pot.

A couple of days later, I was just coming back from a kayak ride up the coast and I saw a brand spanking new black Corvette Lingenfelter convertible parked beside Lucy's Bimmer.

"What a beautiful automobile," I said to myself, then didn't think any more of it. High dollar cars are very common in the San Diego area. I went on up to my condo to clean up and kissed Lucy as I passed by the kitchen table where she was sitting.

"How about some fish and chips?" she asked.

"Sure girl, just let me shower and get some clean clothes."

We walked outside and she flipped me a remote.

"Here."

"I have one," I replied.

"Not like this you don't."

I looked at it and saw a gold Chevy bowtie logo embossed deep into the leather. I pushed the unlock button and amber lights flashed on the new car parked next to Lucy's.

"Did you have enough in your account for this?" I asked.

"Nope, I wrote a check from our corporate account," she said.

I shook my head, smiled, and dropped my new toy down into first. I gently pressed on the gas and we laid rubber all the way up the ramp of the 5, and out into traffic.

"Damn! This is one amazing piece of equipment."

I looked over at Lucy and she was sitting back in her chair. Her eyes were closed, her blond hair was blowing around the very large smile on her beautiful face and the speakers filled the car with the voice of Elvis; 'the night and you and blue Hawaii' and life was very, very good.

To Be Continued...in Vegas!

A ROC REESE MYSTERY
2
BIRDIES
&VEGAS HEAT
In this round,
winning
is everything!
TO Fabulous
LAS VEGAS
NEVADA
DUKE CHARLES

Chapter 1
Practice Swing

Tuesday morning, Barstow, Ca

"Did I do something wrong sheriff?" I asked.

"Did you see anyone else doing 137 miles an hour, Mr. Reese?" the CHP officer asked.

"Do I know you officer?"

"No Roc, but every one in law enforcement in three states, knows who you are."

"Do you need to see my license and carry permit?"

"No, we're good. Where you headed, my friend?"

"Vegas, for a little golf and some of those 99 cent breakfasts," I smiled.

"It's been a while since you've been to Vegas. They're ten or twelve bucks now. Try to keep it down will you? You know we don't really care about you but we sure would hate to see any bruises on Miss Barnes here."

"I hear you, sheriff."

"Just in case, I'll call ahead and let them know your coming."

"Thanks sheriff, I really appreciate it. We have a tee time in 45 minutes."

"But you're still 2 hours...oh, you're messing with me," and he walked off smiling and shaking his head.

He turned off his red and blue flashing lights and made a U turn and headed back south on highway 15. He was about a quarter of a mile away when his car exploded and flew into the air turning back flips and landing on its top.

I looked all around to see where the shot or rocket or whatever it was had come from. I called 911 and there was a chopper from San Bernardino on the scene within twelve minutes. We gave them as much information as we could and then they let us go on our way. So much for our tee time, I guess we'll just sit and drink.

"Those legs are the absolute best thing in the world when it comes to avoiding tickets. Don't you ever let them get flabby as long as I'm alive, Lucy girl."

She smiled and asked, "Just how much longer are you going to be alive?"

I dropped the brand new Corvette Lingenfelter convertible into manual low gear and punched it. Sand and gravel flew and tires squealed and we were up to 142 mph in less than 10 seconds. Lucy laid back in her seat and Elvis sang, 'A Pocketful of Rainbows,' from GI Blues and life was good.

Lucy had made arrangements for our clubs to be delivered to the Wynn. The Vet was just a little cramped for anything more than two cups of Starbucks and a lady's purse, so we were traveling extremely light. The word had got out about the grouchy old guy and the beauty queen that played senior high stakes golf and my phone had been ringing off the hook for the last 3 weeks. This match was with the guy that invented the machine that make aluminum foil and one of his retired buddies/business partners. He had us fixed up in a suite at the Wynn, and had arrangements made for us to play on Stevie's private course; two maybe three rounds depending on the outcome.

We checked into our room; very beautiful. I returned a few calls while Lucy went down and picked up some golf attire for our round this afternoon. The CHP officer weighed on my mind. What was that all about?

The Limo took us to the country club and we met our hosts; Punchy Rains, the aluminum king and Lyle Byrum, a retired movie stunt man. Lyle now considered himself an entreprencur, doing something with race cars out in the desert and flying rich folks all over the country in Lear jets for big bucks.

"You should have said something, I would have flown down to get you in the Lear," Lyle said sounding a little too eager to let us know he had a Lear. Actually, I think he had three of them.

"Not a problem," I said. "We have the Vet and totally enjoyed the drive."

"Yeah, she's hot," Punchy said, "...and so is the car!" and they both laughed.

"Okay, so that's the way it's going to be, down and dirty." I winked at Lucy, "Don't hold back baby doll," and the game was on.

I had played a match at Steve's place with a politician from Utah ten or twelve years back, but it only lasted 15 holes. He walked off the course and I never heard from him again. It has always amazed me how a little thing like $32,000 can break up a brand new friendship.

Lucy shot 76, Punchy shot 78, Lyle shot 74 and I shot 73 when I found out that was all I needed. Two bets on the front and three on the back and we were up 25K, each. The boys laughed and wanted us to meet their ladies and join Steve for dinner. I really wasn't interested, but it seemed like the thing to do to keep them sociable and in the mood to play tomorrow.

"Okay, I'll buy," I said.

"Your damn right you will," Punchy said laughing.

The Prime Rib was amazing, and I have to say and the wine was very special. Lucy and I had been learning more and more about fine wines and pairings and of course we were enjoying the study of it all. But I do think I will always go back to Crown Royal, neat or on the rocks and a cold brew. Occasionally, a Tequila shot may enter the situation.

The bill was marked paid when it came, so I left five, one hundred dollar bills on the table as a tip. We made our way up to our room and before I hit the sheets, I was out. I slept great that night until I heard the Jacuzzi running at about 2am.

"Who's there? And why are you taking a bath in my room?" I asked.

"Go back to sleep, unless you want to join me?"

"You know I can never say no to you."

The next morning the limo picked us up at 8:30 and shuttled us to the course where a private chef fixed our breakfast; two eggs, sausage, ham, bacon and some hash browns and your plate is full. Add to that a Mimosa and some coffee and I was ready to dance.

Punchy and Lyle were both in a great mood when we met them on the first tee. They raised the bet to ten grand and they only lost two bets for the day. They felt like winners; another 40K in the corporate coffers.

"Do you kids mind if we pass on tomorrow? A couple of things have come up that I need to be involved in," Punchy said.

"Not a problem," I said. "We'll probably just head for home in the morning."

Lyle jumped in, "I have a buddy over Dallas way that would love to get some of this action. We can fly over in the morning, play all day and I'll have you back by five in the afternoon. What do you say?"

By 10:30 the next morning, we were teeing it up at the TPC Las Colinas in Irving Texas, home of the Byron Nelson Classic and one of the finest courses anywhere. Lyle's friend, Snuffy Smith was a crazy old man who could hardly hit the ball out of his shadow. Every time he lost a hole he would laugh out loud, reach in his bag and pull out another stack of hundreds and then throw them at Lucy's feet. She just kept looking at me and I kept shrugging, so she kept picking them up and putting them in her bag.

We were winning so much, even I was starting to get a little embarrassed and I missed a couple of bets on the card.

When we finished and we were settling the wagers, I told Snuffy the total, and he got really upset. Ah crap, here we go; one of those guys that can't count and never believes how much he's lost. In Snuffy's case, it was just the opposite.

"What's your problem ol' shoe? You flunk your numbers in school?"

"Well, I never was very good that's for sure," I said. "But I know how to add a scorecard."

"You missed it by 30 grand." he said adding another stack of hundreds to the pile."I can't remember the last time I had that much fun or spent the day with a lady that looks this beautiful. It has been a total pleasure to meet you folks and I hope to run across y'all again soon."

Lucy and I enjoyed our short trip back to Vegas in the Lear. I sat there amazed at the luxury and I guess it was obvious. I looked at Lucy and she was watching me.

"You want one, don't you?" she laughed.

"Yeah, I really do," I said.

As we made our final approach into McCarran International Airport, Lucy and I were strapped in and ready to get back on the ground. It would be nice to enjoy a little dinner, a cocktail or two and some sleep before we headed for home in the morning. We were coming in at what seemed to be a normal descent when all of a sudden the Lear jerked hard right and headed up at about 65 degree angle. We were forced back in our seats and we stared at each other with just a little concern on our faces. I could see Lyle's shoulders and head through the open cabin door and he was pulling hard on the stick. When we finally leveled off, I unbuckled my seatbelt and moved forward. I could hear Lyle on the intercom.

"Tower, this is Byrum 114; someone from your tower is blinding me with a laser. Can you get that under control? Over."

"Sorry about that, Captain. We saw it too. Security is on it now and should have the situation under control right away. Get back into formation and we'll get you down as quickly as possible."

"Roger that. Hang in their Roc, I'm gonna put this thing down and go kick some ass."

I strapped myself into the right seat and put the headphones on.

"You Okay, Skipper?" I asked.

"Yeah, I'm fine. Luckily I wear these shades all the time or you might be landing this thing."

"I'd hate to think of that scenario. I just barely passed my last drivers test," I replied.

"Some kid is gonna be wearing my size 11 boot in his ass when I get in there."

We landed, got into the limo and headed for the hotel. It took about 10 minutes till we were getting out and heading for our room.

"What do you think about room service tonight?" I asked.

"Sounds good to me, I'm a little worn myself. I'm gonna take a Jacuzzi and have a very large Crown, so don't order dinner too soon," Lucy said.

I poured myself a Crown in a large tumbler and dropped a chunk of ice on top and all of a sudden fatigue began to set in.

"You got room in there for me?" I asked.

"Always, my dear!"

Wow, she looked amazing. I will never get tired of this view. The phone rang and I tried to work my way through the bubbles. I guess I had dozed off.

"Hello!"

"Roc?" the strange voice asked.

"Yes, this is Roc Reese. What can I do for you?"

"Roc, its Lyle."

"Yeah, Lyle what's wrong?"

There was silence for a few seconds.

"Roc, its Terry, my wife, she's dead..."

More silence.

"She's been shot."

More to come in...

BIRDIES & VEGAS HEAT

A Roc Reese Mystery

DUKE CHARLES

Birdies & Vegas Heat

Coming soon to
Amazon, Barnes & Noble and
Everywhere great fiction is sold.

Find out more at DukeCharles.com

Other Books by Duke Charles

LUKE KASH WESTERN SERIES

People of the Horse
Spirit and the Blood
Blood and Thunder
Thunder Cloud and Spirit Walker

ROC REESE MYSTERY SERIES

Birdies and San Diego Heat
Birdies and Vegas Heat
Birdies and Texas Heat
Birdies and New Orleans Heat

Gideon, Bounty Hunter
Duke Charles' Shorts
Duke Charles' Shorts-Another Stinkin' Pair

When I Grow Up I Want To Be A Cowboy
Written with Brad Engel

46390976R00140

Made in the USA
San Bernardino, CA
06 March 2017